A very difficult situation . . .

"Ashleigh?" Cindy called. "Can I ask you something?"

"Yes, Cindy?" Ashleigh said as she walked back toward the feed room.

Cindy twisted her hands nervously. "Is Shining going to run in the Classic?" she asked.

Ashleigh's brow furrowed. "So you still don't know? You should talk to Sammy about it," Ashleigh said firmly, scooping oats into Secret Silence's bucket. She picked up the bucket and headed back down the aisle.

Cindy trailed behind her. "But Sammy's already left for the track," she said miserably.

"Call her," Ashleigh said over her shoulder.

I can't. Cindy sat down on a hay bale in front of Storm's stall. *What would I say to Sammy if I called her?* Cindy wondered. *"I hope you're not running Shining in the Classic because I want my horse to win?" That sounds so selfish. But I have been selfish,* Cindy realized. *It's probably too late now to straighten things out with her. I should have talked to her about this weeks ago.*

Collect all the books in the Thoroughbred series

Collect all the books in the Ashleigh series

* coming soon

THOROUGHBRED

GLORY'S RIVAL

CREATED BY
JOANNA CAMPBELL

WRITTEN BY
KAREN BENTLEY
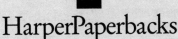
BILLINGS COUNTY PUBLIC SCHOOL
Box 307
Medora, North Dakota 58645

HarperPaperbacks
A Division of HarperCollins*Publishers*

HarperPaperbacks
A Division of HarperCollinsPublishers
10 East 53rd Street, New York, N.Y. 10022-5299

This is a work of fiction. The characters, incidents, and dialogues are products of the author's imagination and are not to be construed as real. Any resemblance to actual events or persons, living or dead, is entirely coincidental.

ISBN 0-06-106398-3

HarperCollins®, 📖 ®, and HarperPaperbacks™ are trademarks of HarperCollinsPublishers Inc.

First printing: January 1997

Printed in the United States of America

Visit HarperPaperbacks on the World Wide Web at
http://www.harpercollins.com

❖ 10 9 8 7 6

To John

With special thanks to Barbara Vande Sande

GLORY'S RIVAL

1

"JUST STAND QUIETLY, STORM," CINDY MCLEAN SAID AS SHE eased her weight over the colt's back in his stall, the first step in breaking him to a saddle. "That's a perfect boy."

The beautiful dark gray yearling, Storm's Ransom, snorted and nervously sidestepped, tossing his elegant, perfectly shaped head. Len, the stable manager at Whitebrook, the successful Thoroughbred breeding and training farm in Kentucky where Cindy lived, rubbed the colt's neck reassuringly. "This guy's always a gentleman," he said. "I bet we won't have any real trouble with him all down the line to running him on the track."

"Yeah, but Storm's feisty today," Heather Gilbert commented. "Maybe because he likes fall weather." Heather, Cindy's best friend and in the seventh grade like Cindy, often came over to Whitebrook to ride and help Cindy with the horses. That afternoon they were exercising Storm and enjoying the cool, crisp October air.

"He sure feels good. But you're just a baby, aren't you?" Cindy soothed the colt. She lay as still as she could, her blond hair spilling over Storm's glossy, smooth back. Storm was a gentle colt, but Cindy could feel the tension in all his muscles. "Remember, we've done this before," she reminded him. In training him, Cindy always repeated Storm's lessons. So far she had rubbed his ears and legs, put on the bridle and light exercise saddle, lain across the colt's back, and while up in the saddle walked him around the yearling ring behind Len.

"Today's such a big day, Storm," Cindy murmured. "Behave yourself." If all went well, she planned to try riding the colt alone in the yearling ring, without Len's steadying hand leading him.

The young gray horse bounced lightly on his front legs. He wasn't quite rearing, but Cindy hung on tightly, every nerve in her body ready to respond to the colt's next move. She knew that breaking a young horse was risky. Storm could go up, injuring his head on the ceiling, or lash out at the sides of the stall and break a leg. If he moved quickly and caught her by surprise, she could be thrown and hurt by the panicking young horse's hooves.

But I'm not afraid of you, she thought, communicating

2

her feelings to the colt through her gentle touch. Cindy had grown close to Storm's Ransom in the six weeks since Whitebrook had bought him at the Saratoga yearling sale in mid-August. She was sure she could handle the lively colt. And most of all, Cindy was sure that training him was a wonderful, worthwhile thing to do. She was just twelve, and she knew that she was incredibly lucky to have the opportunity.

Ashleigh Griffen, Whitebrook's co-owner with her husband, Mike Reese, was expecting a baby in January and had temporarily given up riding. Mike and Ian McLean, Cindy's father and head trainer at Whitebrook, had been training at the Belmont track since the early summer.

Because everyone else was busy, Cindy had volunteered to help train Storm's Ransom. Cindy had felt an immediate bond with the dark gray colt the moment she first saw him, right after the auction. Storm had been trembling with uncertainty but still walking quietly behind his handler, doing his best to adjust to the new circumstances.

"Steady, now," Len said, gently tugging on Storm's lead rope. "Ease off him," he advised Cindy, still rubbing the colt's neck. "I think he's had enough for now."

Cindy slowly slid down off the colt until her boots touched the stall floor. Storm gave a snort and swung his head around to look at her quizzically.

"It's just me," Cindy said with a laugh. "I'm the

3

same whether I'm on your back or beside you. That's what we're trying to teach you, Storm."

The young horse lowered his head and looked at her dubiously, as if to say, *Are you sure?*

"Do you really think you can ride him alone today?" Heather asked.

"Yes," Cindy said. Len was already giving her a hand up over the colt's back again. "Sometimes Storm forgets what he's learned for a minute or two, but he always remembers." Cindy had been training the colt for six weeks, since she had returned from Saratoga right after the August yearling sale.

The summer meet at the Saratoga track had finished in triumph for Whitebrook. Cindy smiled as she remembered how March to Glory, the dapple gray colt she had rescued from thieves and persuaded Mike to buy and race, had won the grade-one Travers in the teeth of a headwind of forty miles per hour. Glory was now a contender for the Breeders' Cup Classic, the richest race of the year, at the end of October.

Shining, the prize red roan filly belonging to Samantha McLean, Cindy's eighteen-year-old adoptive sister, had run a brilliant race in the Whitney at Saratoga in August. Because Shining had done so well against colts in the Whitney, Samantha was undecided whether Shining would race next in the Breeders' Cup Distaff, for fillies and mares, or in the Breeders' Cup Classic, against Glory and other colts.

This year the Breeders' Cup races would be run at the Belmont track in New York, where Shining, Glory, and the rest of the Whitebrook string were currently racing.

Again Cindy carefully slid onto Storm's back. This time the colt tolerated her weight. He huffed out a little sigh, then stood completely still, as if he was awaiting Cindy's commands.

Cindy felt a rush of pure pleasure. "Attaboy," she praised. She had been sure Storm would be all right that day. So far in Storm's training she had been right most of the time about what he would do, and she knew that Len and Ashleigh were pleased with her work. But sometimes Cindy could hardly believe that Mike, Ashleigh, and Ian had taken her up on her offer to help train the colt.

"I'll go get the saddle and bridle," Len said as Cindy slid off again. "I think he's ready."

"I do, too," Cindy said confidently. She threw her arms around Storm's neck, partly to get him used to the sudden motion but mostly just because he deserved a hug. The colt nuzzled her pockets quizzically.

"I think he wants a carrot," Heather said with a laugh.

"Not yet, Storm." Cindy took the colt's exercise saddle from Len and with practiced hands positioned it and tightened the girth.

"I'll lead you and Storm over to the walking ring," Len said. "Then I'll turn you loose."

Cindy nodded, tightening the strap on her helmet. Outside the barn she quickly mounted up with a hand from Len—at almost sixteen hands Storm was already a tall colt. Storm calmly followed Len to the yearling ring, a structure with six-foot-high wood walls to minimize distractions to the young horses. In the confined space the yearlings were also easier to control.

A brisk wind blew the first fallen leaves under Storm's hooves. Cindy squinted into the bright yellow sun, enjoying its pleasant warmth on her face. She bent to adjust the stirrup irons on her feet.

"Hey, you guys." Ashleigh walked over from the front paddock to join them. "How's it going?"

"Great," Cindy said happily. Storm danced lightly after Len, as if he couldn't wait to get to the walking ring and to work.

"Storm's turning into a beautiful horse," Ashleigh commented. Her hazel eyes narrowed as she studied the colt intently.

Cindy thought Ashleigh sounded wistful. Six months pregnant and wearing maternity clothes, Ashleigh was restricted to training these days. Cindy knew that although Ashleigh was excited about the baby, she missed riding. Ashleigh was a renowned jockey who at the age of sixteen had ridden Ashleigh's Wonder, winner of the Kentucky Derby, to a victory in the Breeders' Cup Classic.

Wonder had been retired years ago after breaking a

cannon bone, but she had proven to be a superb broodmare. Her first son, Wonder's Pride, had been named Horse of the Year before he colicked and was retired to stud. Mr. Wonderful, her two-year-old son, was now at the Belmont track. He had recovered from a strained tendon and would run in the Champagne Stakes the same day that Glory ran in his next race, the Jockey Club Gold Cup, in just three days.

"How's Wonder's Champion?" Cindy asked Ashleigh. Cindy was sure Ashleigh had just been admiring Wonder's five-month-old colt, who was out in the front paddock with Wonder. Wonder's Champion was the most promising colt at Whitebrook.

Ashleigh laughed. "Do you need to ask? You know how I feel about Wonder's foals. I think our champ is going to be Whitebrook's first Triple Crown winner. He's become such a big, sturdy fellow already. We'll have to wean him soon."

Cindy tightened up on the reins as Storm's Ransom jumped over a small whirlwind of blowing leaves. She reached to stroke his neck. "Nothing to worry about," she said.

The colt settled down again and moved in a straight line after Len, rolling his prominent dark eyes backward to watch Cindy. Cindy had always loved the way horses could keep their eyes on someone without even turning their heads.

"I don't know about this guy," Ashleigh said,

patting Storm's flank as the colt pranced by her. "He's a wild card."

Cindy knew that Storm's breeding wasn't all that distinguished. Mike and Ian had bought the colt because they thought the particular cross of his dam and sire looked good for a sprinter. Usually sprinters ran races of only six or seven furlongs. "He's going well now," Cindy protested.

"I know. Mike's had more experience with sprinters than I have, and he's got a lot of confidence in Storm," Ashleigh confirmed.

In the yearling ring Len led the colt for a few paces, then released the reins. He, Heather, and Ashleigh gathered at the center of the ring to watch.

"This is your big moment," Cindy murmured to the colt. "I hope you're as ready for it as I think you are."

She squeezed with her legs, asking Storm to walk. The young horse hesitated, as if he wondered where Len was, then moved out briskly. Cindy guided him in a circle, following the wall of the ring. She could feel the uncertainty of Storm's movements compared to those of a more finished horse such as Glory.

Storm drifted in from the circle. Patiently Cindy corrected him with the reins, pulling his head slightly around. *Storm has to learn everything, even to walk in a circle*, she reminded herself. *He wasn't born knowing that.*

After one circuit Cindy stopped the colt and rubbed his sides with her legs. He stood quietly, as Cindy expected. None of her actions were new to the young horse. The only new thing was that they were doing everything themselves, Cindy thought. A thrill flushed her cheeks.

"He couldn't be doing better," Ashleigh called from the center of the ring. "Try a trot with him."

Cindy clucked to the colt, asking him for the faster pace. Storm responded instantly, even trotting at the exact speed she had tried to cue him for. *This is so cool!* Cindy exulted. She was excited about how well she and the colt were doing, but she cautioned herself not to let her concentration break for a second. From exercise-riding Glory, Cindy knew how alert and skilled she needed to be to control a young, high-powered Thoroughbred.

Storm gave his head a spirited toss. The next second he tried to break out of the trot into a gallop. "No, you don't," Cindy said, pulling his head around and easing back simultaneously on the reins to slow him. She expertly gauged just how much pressure she needed to apply. Too much would hurt the colt, and eventually he might develop a hard mouth. And pulling his head around too sharply could make him lose his balance and fall on her.

Soon Storm was trotting smoothly again, as if nothing had happened. "That's good for today," Ashleigh called after they had made several circuits. "Very nice, Cindy."

Beaming at Ashleigh's praise, Cindy dismounted and led Storm out of the ring. Storm stopped at the gate and pushed his muzzle into her hair. He took a deep breath and shook himself.

"Yes, it's really you and me doing such wonderful work," Cindy said with a laugh, running a hand over his straight, smooth gray back. "I can hardly believe it, either. You're almost a racehorse."

"That was great," Heather said as they walked the colt around the stable yard to cool him out. Storm pranced behind Cindy with mincing steps. Obviously the exercise hadn't taken anything out of him.

"Yeah, I think so, too. I just hope he doesn't forget everything he's learned while I'm in New York." Cindy frowned. "Sammy, Ashleigh, and I leave for Belmont on Friday so that we can be with Glory for the Jockey Club Gold Cup on Saturday. That means I've got only two days left with Storm."

"He won't forget," Heather said reassuringly. "He's smart. And you won't be gone long."

"Just Friday, Saturday, and Sunday. I'm counting the minutes until I see Glory again." For a second Cindy stopped Storm in his tracks, thinking longingly of Glory, her very favorite horse. "I miss Glory so much," she added.

Cindy wondered for the thousandth time how Glory was really doing. She knew she had reason to worry. Just before Glory's stunning victory in the

Travers, Ashleigh had been forced to sell a half interest in him to the Townsends, the owners of Townsend Acres, a huge breeding and training farm. Ashleigh and the Townsends were co-owners of Wonder and all her offspring, an arrangement dating to when Ashleigh had made a champion of Wonder for Townsend Acres. They now owned half of Wonder's Champion and wanted to train him at Townsend Acres. The only way Ashleigh had been able to persuade the Townsends to let Wonder's Champion stay at Whitebrook for his training was to sell them the half interest in Glory.

Cindy knew that the Townsends, as co-owners of Glory, legitimately had a say in his training and racing schedules. But because Glory was doing so well on the track, Ashleigh had hoped the Townsends wouldn't interfere with him.

It hadn't worked out that way, Cindy remembered with a frown. Brad Townsend, who increasingly managed the affairs of Townsend Acres while his father, Clay Townsend, supervised the family businesses overseas, was difficult to deal with, and he had never liked Ashleigh. He and his wife, Lavinia, had sniped nonstop at Ashleigh, Mike, and Ian about Glory's training from the first day they'd become co-owners of the colt. Ashleigh hadn't liked most of their training ideas.

"I wish I could go with you to Belmont," Heather

said wistfully, running a hand through Storm's silvery mane.

"It would be a lot more fun if you could." *And maybe you could help me keep an eye on the Townsends,* Cindy thought. But she doubted if Heather could ever go to a track so far from Kentucky. Heather came from a big family, and her parents probably couldn't afford to send her just for fun. *I'm lucky I have real work to do at the track,* Cindy thought. Everyone at Whitebrook accepted that because she and Glory had such a special bond, the colt did better when she was around. "We can go to races this fall at Keeneland and Churchill Downs," Cindy said quickly.

"Yeah, that'll be fun." Heather smiled.

Storm was looking at the barn. Cindy could hear feed buckets clanging and the whinnies of eager horses. "I know, it's dinnertime," she said. She felt the colt's chest to see if he was too warm and looked at her watch to check how long they had been walking. "You should be completely cooled out by now, boy. Okay, let's go!"

Storm needed no further urging. The gray colt tugged Cindy into Whitebrook's biggest barn, where the farm's fifteen horses in training were stabled.

Imp, Glory's cat friend, was pacing on the half door of Glory's stall. The young gray and white cat had adopted Glory soon after the colt had come to Whitebrook, and the two animals had become almost inseparable. But with Glory away at the track so much that summer and fall, Imp seemed lost. He spent most of his time hanging around Glory's stall, apparently hoping his horse companion would return.

The moment Imp saw Storm, he jumped off the stall door and ran down the aisle, his tail hiked straight in the air. Cindy noticed with amusement that Imp wouldn't have anything to do with the newcomer.

"I guess all gray horses aren't the same, huh?" she called after the cat. Imp froze before the barn door, sniffing the chilly evening breeze. He darted into Shining's empty stall.

"He likes Shining's stall second best after Glory's," Heather said with a laugh.

"So do I." Cindy was Shining's groom and knew every inch of Samantha's superb filly.

Cindy glanced down the aisle, noticing how many stall doors swung open to reveal empty stalls. *So many of the horses are gone—Glory, Shining, Mr. Wonderful*, she thought.

"What's the matter?" Heather asked. "You look sad."

"Oh, I just miss the horses—especially Glory. It's hard not to be able to say good night to him." When Glory was home, every night Cindy caught him up on the events of the day. Even though she knew Glory couldn't understand her words, he would listen intently to the sound of her voice. Cindy had begun to love Storm, too, but she knew it would take time for her to feel nearly as much for him as she did for Glory.

"Glory and Shining are at the track," Heather pointed out. "So they're not really gone."

"I know." Cindy opened the door to Storm's stall and let the impatient colt go. "It's absolutely great that my favorite horses are at Belmont," Cindy continued. "Soon Glory and Shining will be running in some of the biggest races in the world. They wouldn't be gone if they hadn't run fantastic races this summer. But I still feel lonesome without them."

"I guess you would. Wow, Storm's hungry," Heather remarked. Storm was restlessly pacing, stopping after each circuit to look out the door.

"Yeah, he's still growing a lot. And not just taller— the exercise is making him fill out." Cindy cast a critical eye over Storm. In the near dark he was a glossy, rich gray, the color of fine pewter.

Storm snorted impatiently, as if to say, *Aren't you ever going to stop admiring me and feed me?*

"I'm going!" Cindy laughed as she grabbed an empty bucket and hurried to the feed room.

"My mom's here," Heather called. "I'd better go. See you tomorrow in school."

"Okay." Cindy frowned as she measured out Storm's dinner. School really got in the way sometimes, she thought. Early that morning it had rained, and so she'd been forced to work with Storm after school instead of first thing in the morning. That had upset his training routine. Cindy was sure it was one reason he'd been jumpy at first that afternoon.

Oh, well—Storm did fine after a while, she said to herself as she carried the heavy bucket back to the waiting colt. *I guess I can't make everything perfect for him.*

Cindy poured the grain into Storm's tray and watched fondly for several moments as he dug in. "Good night, boy," she said. "I'll see you tomorrow, bright and early." The big colt looked up briefly, then returned to his supper.

Cindy headed for the mares' barn to visit Wonder and Wonder's Champion. Ashleigh wasn't the only one who thought the young horse had amazing prospects. Cindy thought he was bigger and more beautiful every day.

The dark chestnut colt was munching hay in a stall with Wonder. When he saw Cindy, he stepped over to the stall door, eagerly flicking his short tail. "You think I'm a better treat than hay?" Cindy teased. "Thanks."

Wonder looked up, too, her intelligent eyes soft with recognition. Cindy was struck again by how much Wonder's Champion resembled his dam. Except for his coat color, he looked exactly like pictures Cindy had seen of Wonder as a foal.

Cindy stepped into the stall and sandwiched herself between the two horses, petting both outstretched noses and the soft copper and mahogany necks. To

Cindy, Wonder's Champion looked taller and more filled out than most five-month-old colts. And his legs seemed to be set at just the right angle to maximize the speed of his strides.

"You're such a special horse," she murmured. "I can't be mad at Ashleigh about selling the half interest in Glory to the Townsends. We have to keep you here."

"Let's try to make the best of the new situation with Glory," Ashleigh had said that summer, but she had looked unhappy. "Since Wonder's Champion is untried, the Townsends may have gotten something for nothing—we know Glory can run. But until Wonder's Champion gets out on the track, there's no telling how well he'll do."

Cindy looked at the exquisite colt. Wonder's Champion was energetically bumping the feed tray with his nose, searching for every last grain. Already his muscles rippled under his smooth dark coat, and with his proud arched neck he looked every bit the young racehorse. Whenever Cindy saw Wonder's Champion, she was positive she'd picked out the perfect name for him.

"Ashleigh gave the Townsends a lot for you," Cindy said to the colt. "But I really think you'll be worth it. You just might be the farm's greatest champion yet."

2

CINDY HAD LIVED AT WHITEBROOK FOR OVER A YEAR, BUT she thought she would never get used to how beautiful it was. As she walked up the path to her family's cottage for dinner, Cindy was sure that the day the McLeans adopted her had been the luckiest day of her life.

The clear fall twilight brushed Mike and Ashleigh's old white farmhouse with a blue-gray color, and the training, mares', and stallions' barns were a dusky, deep red. Sometimes Cindy could hardly believe that she lived on a farm with thirty pedigreed, gorgeous Thoroughbreds and a loving, warm family. She had been in foster care most of her life after her parents were killed in a car accident.

Cindy walked through the hall into the kitchen of her family's cottage, sniffing a warm, delicious scent. "Sammy! Are you cooking dinner?" she asked in surprise.

Samantha set down a package of potatoes and laughed. She wore a dark green apron that went well with her red hair and green eyes. "Your jaw's dropping! Who says I can't cook?"

"Nobody. It's just that you usually don't."

"Beth had to teach an evening class tonight, remember?" Beth McLean, Samantha's stepmother and Cindy's adoptive mother, ran an aerobics business in Lexington.

"You should have called me to help," Cindy said. Beth, a gourmet cook, always took charge in the kitchen. But Cindy was sure Samantha could manage. Samantha's mother had died in a riding accident when Samantha was twelve. Cindy supposed that before Ian and Beth had married, the summer before last, Samantha had often cooked for her dad and herself.

"I'm doing okay here. Anyway, you seemed to have your hands full with Storm. How's he coming along?" Samantha asked as she deftly sliced a potato. "I wish I had more time to help you with his training, but college is a full-time job." Samantha was a sophomore at the University of Kentucky.

"Storm's doing great. He's just so smart and friendly." Cindy smiled at the remembrance of the sweet trust in Storm's dark eyes.

"The people we bought him from at Saratoga are small breeders," Samantha said. "They take a personal

18

interest in their horses. That's probably why he's so nice."

"Probably." Cindy picked up a potato peeler and looked uncertainly at the pile of green peppers Samantha had prepared. "What is this?"

"Hungarian goulash. Tor's coming over, so I wanted to make something special," Samantha said, referring to her longtime boyfriend, Tor Nelson. Tor and his father ran a jumping stable near Lexington. Tor was also the jockey of Sierra, Whitebrook's star steeplechaser.

Cindy heard a knock. "I bet that's him," she said, hurrying to open the door.

"Hey, Cindy." Blond, tall Tor Nelson gave her a warm smile. "Hi, Sammy," he said, coming into the kitchen and kissing Samantha's cheek. "Sorry I'm late—I was putting Sierra over a few jumps."

"You're not late—you're just in time to make the fruit salad for dessert," Samantha said with a grin. "Everything you need is in the refrigerator."

"Fine with me." Tor looked appreciatively over Samantha's shoulder at the pot of goulash. With Cindy's help he cut up apples, tangerines, a honeydew melon, and a cantaloupe to put together a luscious fruit salad.

"The main course is ready." Samantha moved to the stove and turned off the heat under the simmering goulash. Samantha and Tor served up the steaming, colorful dish while Cindy finished setting the table. Then they all sat down to eat.

"This is great, Sammy," Cindy said after she had tasted the goulash.

"Mmm," Tor said, filling his fork again. "I agree."

"It did turn out pretty well," Samantha admitted. "I'm just a little surprised."

"I'm not." Tor put his hand over Samantha's.

"I'm not, either—Sammy can do anything she tries," Cindy said affectionately. "Look at Shining." Samantha had transformed an abused, scared, half-starved filly into a brilliant racehorse.

"How are Shining and the other horses at Belmont doing?" Tor asked.

"Shining's fine." Samantha smiled fondly. "She's a real pro. Of course, I have to make a major decision soon—whether to run her in the Distaff or the Classic."

Cindy looked quickly at Samantha, hoping she would go on talking. If Shining ran in the Classic, Shining and Glory would be rivals. Cindy didn't feel good about that prospect. Ever since Samantha had mentioned the possibility after Shining's victory in the Whitney in August, Cindy had been wondering what Samantha would decide.

"Shining's getting a good rest. She'll be ready for the Breeders' Cup, whichever race she runs in," Tor said to Samantha.

"I hope so," Samantha said. "I suppose I could have

run her before then, like in the Beldame next Saturday. But I still think I did the right thing by letting her rest." Samantha looked thoughtful. "She's going to need to be at the top of her game to compete in the Breeders' Cup."

Cindy knew that Shining stood a good chance of doing well in the Classic. Shining was one of the best fillies in the world. She had beaten the colts resoundingly in two major races, the Suburban and the Whitney, and newspaper articles had compared her to Ruffian, the greatest filly of all time. A win in the Classic for Shining would be fantastic.

Samantha will probably enter Shining in the Classic, Cindy thought. *But I want Glory to win it!* Cindy hoped he would set a world record or at least a track record in the race. Cindy wanted Glory to rival Just Victory, his grandsire and one of the fastest horses ever. Just Victory had won some races by almost a quarter mile.

"Shining should hold her own in the Breeders' Cup," Tor said.

"Yes, I think so, too," Samantha agreed. "She drilled five furlongs at Belmont yesterday."

"Shining's absolutely the greatest," Cindy said quickly. She meant that, but she felt guilty. She wanted Glory to win—but she knew that meant Shining would lose!

Samantha looked at Cindy intently, then shook her head and changed the subject. "I'll come over tomorrow to help you with Sierra," she told Tor.

"Thanks—I could use it," Tor replied.

Cindy continued to eat, but she hardly tasted the delicious food now. *Sammy and I have such a great relationship,* she thought, watching Samantha and Tor talk animatedly about how they would condition Sierra. *But how would either of us feel if our horse lost the Classic?*

"Do you want to go on a trail ride after school?" Cindy asked Heather the next morning as she shut her locker at Henry Clay Middle School. The hall was packed with kids rushing to their classes before the final bell rang. Cindy knew she should hurry, too, but she was reluctant to start the school day.

Storm had outdone himself in their training session early that morning. The colt had followed the slightest leg and hand signals as Cindy rode him alone. He seemed to know what Cindy wanted even before she asked for it. Riding the quick, sensitive young horse just after dawn under a cold pink sun, Cindy had laughed from sheer triumph. But now her mind was still at Whitebrook even more than usual.

"Of course I want to go for a trail ride—do you have to ask?" Heather grinned.

"Maybe we can ask Mandy to come, too," Cindy added as she and Heather walked to homeroom. Mandy Jarvis was only eight, but she was an excellent all-around rider. Cindy and Heather had gotten to know Mandy when she was a member of the Pony Commandos, a group of disabled riders Tor and Samantha coached at Tor's stable. Mandy still wore metal leg braces, but the doctors were optimistic that she would get them off soon. Because of her riding talent Mandy had graduated from the Pony Commandos to private jumping lessons with Tor. She now competed in shows against nondisabled riders.

"That'd be fun if Mandy went with us," Heather said. "I'll call her as soon as I get home."

"But we still have to get through the whole school day." Cindy groaned. Cindy was a straight-A student, and usually she liked school. But it was hard to fit in training, riding, and chores on school days. Cindy had trouble finishing her work with the horses, especially with Storm, before school started, and the early fall darkness cut short her time after school, too. *I really hope Storm doesn't turn into a wild horse while I'm at Belmont and no one's riding him*, she thought.

The morning flew by, even though Cindy had feared it would drag. Just before lunch she had her favorite class, science.

Cindy walked to the lab table that she shared with Max Smith, her lab partner and good friend. "Hi, Max," she greeted him.

"Hey, Cindy. I've got our experiment all set up," Max said. Cindy remembered that in class that day they were going to determine the melting points of unknown substances.

"Looks good." Cindy wasn't surprised that Max had quickly set up the complicated arrangement of beakers, test tubes, and rubber hoses. He was an excellent science student, just as she was. They both dreamed of someday becoming veterinarians. Cindy hoped to combine that career with riding.

Cindy looked at the narrow test tube that held their unknown substance. It was clamped to a stand and hung over a Bunsen burner. "It's already starting to melt." She grabbed her notebook and wrote down the temperature. "So we're done." Cindy sat back in her chair and looked around the room. The rest of her classmates were still setting up the experiment.

Max sat beside her. "Did you ride Storm this morning?" he asked.

"Yeah. He did great. But tomorrow will be my last session with him before I leave for Belmont."

Max laughed. "I can't feel *too* sorry for you!"

"I know, I know." Cindy smiled. "Hey, how's your new horse doing?" Dr. Smith, Max's mother and Whitebrook's veterinarian, reconditioned Thoroughbred and Quarter-Horse racehorses as pleasure horses and barrel racers. The previous weekend Dr. Smith had claimed another horse, Run for It, from one of the smaller Thoroughbred tracks.

"He's settling in," Max said. "He didn't do too well

24

at first. We were worried about him—he just sort of stood around, hanging his head. I think he knew that he was a flop at the track. Run for It's got great bloodlines, but he didn't seem to want to be a racehorse. Every time he was asked to run, he dropped off the bit and drifted out. Mom's thinking he might make a good trail horse."

"I wonder how you can make him feel better," Cindy said.

"Mom already figured that out." Max grinned. "She got him a goat for company. You should see them together—the goat butts Run for It all the time. But he seems to love it."

"I'd like to see them," Cindy said. "I'll definitely come over as soon as I can. I'm just so busy with Storm and Glory right now."

"I know. I'll give you progress reports until you can get there."

"Thanks." Cindy leaned back comfortably in her chair, enjoying imagining the horse and goat together. She knew that goats were common companions for high-strung Thoroughbreds. The two very different kinds of animals often got along well.

Mr. Fox, Cindy's science teacher, approached them from the front of the classroom. "What melting point did you two get for your unknown?" he asked.

"Fifty-two degrees Celsius," Cindy said.

The teacher consulted a list and nodded. "That's

about right. Let's hear about your experimental protocol."

"I'll describe the first half," Max said.

It's nice that Max has horses, Cindy thought as Max began to explain to the teacher how they had done the experiment. *He understands what I'm doing with Storm and doesn't get mad when I can't come over right away.*

After science Cindy hurried to the cafeteria to reserve the special table where she and Heather always sat. It had a view of a park across the street, with beautiful old shade trees. Best of all, Cindy thought, occasionally someone cantered a pleasure horse across the smooth, rolling acres of grass.

"Can we sit with you?" Sharon Rodgers asked just as Cindy was opening her lunch bag.

Cindy looked up and saw Laura Billings and Melissa Souter, two other girls in her class, waiting behind Sharon. Cindy was a little surprised that Sharon and her friends wanted to sit with her. They were cheerleaders and usually hung with the popular crowd. "Sure, I guess," Cindy said. "Okay, Heather?"

Heather, who was just sitting down, nodded. "Fine with me."

"What's new at Whitebrook?" Sharon asked. She sounded a little envious. Cindy knew that with Glory and Shining doing so well at the track, both horses—

and the people at Whitebrook, including herself—were often in the news.

"Not much. I work Storm's Ransom under saddle every morning," Cindy said. "He's the dark gray colt we bought at the Saratoga select yearling sale. Ashleigh and Mike, the owners of Whitebrook, let me call myself Storm's trainer, even though officially Mike is." Cindy stopped herself, realizing that she might be bragging. She didn't mean to show off. It was just so exciting to her that Storm was doing well under her training.

"How do you stay on a young horse like that?" Laura asked. "I can't always keep my legs steady, even on older horses." Cindy knew that Laura often exercise-rode horses at Melissa's. The Souters owned a large breeding and training farm near Lexington.

"It's hard to say what's wrong without seeing you ride, but you could check whether your stirrups are on the ball of your foot," Cindy said. "Sometimes when I first started riding Glory, my stirrups used to slip back, and then I couldn't grip the saddle right."

"I'll look," Laura said. "Thanks, Cindy."

"Next time I don't know what to do with a horse, I'll just ask you." Melissa laughed.

"We really should swap horse stories every day," Cindy said, half joking.

"Well, why don't we?" Sharon asked. "We could sit together a couple of times a week and talk about horses, like Glory and Storm's Ransom. Most of us live on horse farms or are around horses a lot."

Cindy thought about Sharon's suggestion. She did like the idea of talking about horses at lunch. And if they didn't sit together every day, she and Heather would still be able to have lunch alone sometimes and talk privately. "Sounds good to me," she said.

"Yeah, to me, too," Heather agreed.

Cindy spotted Max sitting at a nearby table with his friends. "Let's ask Max to join us," Cindy suggested. "His mom's a vet and a trainer. He does a lot of interesting stuff with horses when he helps her."

"Sure," said Sharon.

"I'll ask him right now." *This will be a fun way to spend lunch*, Cindy thought as she slowly threaded her way toward Max's table in the crowded lunchroom. *I bet Max will think so, too.*

3

"COME ON, SLOWPOKES!" MANDY JARVIS CALLED, GLANCING impatiently over her shoulder. She and Butterball, her spirited caramel-colored pony, had trotted ahead of Heather and Cindy on the trail. The girls were taking the horses on a ride through the woods behind Whitebrook. Mr. Jarvis had trailered Butterball over to Whitebrook after school so that Mandy could ride him with Cindy and Heather. "You guys are riding Thoroughbreds, but you can't even keep up with Butter!" Mandy teased, reining in her small, prancing pony.

Cindy laughed and reached to stroke Wonder's Pride's silken copper neck. Ashleigh had suggested that Cindy take Whitebrook's champion stallion out on the trails that day to exercise him. Cindy was happy to—she loved riding Pride. He was spirited, but he had good trail manners and willingly obeyed her commands.

29

"I guess I could catch you in about a stride if I wanted to, Mandy," Cindy said, letting Pride walk a little faster. "Any Thoroughbred could, but Pride isn't just any Thoroughbred. He won the Breeders' Cup Classic and was Horse of the Year."

Thrilling as riding at speed was, Cindy wasn't in a hurry to move Pride out faster than a walk. She was enjoying just being outdoors on such a beautiful day. The changing leaves of the trees were bright splashes of red, green, and yellow against a clear blue sky. The October late afternoon was mild, with only a chilly nip in the air.

"I guess Pride did run kind of fast to win the Breeders' Cup," Mandy said as Cindy and Pride approached. Mandy's dark eyes were sparkling with mischief.

"He ran *very* fast." Cindy looked thoughtfully at Pride's glossy, broad shoulders, remembering his run in the Classic. Pride's Classic had been several years before Cindy came to Whitebrook, but she had seen videos of it. In a magnificent stretch drive Pride had just edged out the Townsends' horse, Lord Ainsley.

Lord Ainsley had been Lavinia Townsend's special horse, imported from Britain. Cindy doubted if Lavinia had ever forgiven Whitebrook for Pride's win. She certainly acted as if she bore a grudge.

"Pride's not going fast now," Mandy reminded Cindy with a grin.

"I don't want him to." Cindy looked around for

Heather. She was up on Bo Jangles, the trustworthy gelding she usually rode on trail rides at Whitebrook. Cindy couldn't see them around a bend in the trail.

Butterball pawed the ground with one small hoof, as if he was as impatient as Mandy to get going. His dark, intelligent eyes were almost hidden by his shaggy forelock.

"Why don't you be a jockey, Mandy? You're small enough," Cindy teased. "Then you can race all the time."

"I'm only eight—I'll get bigger. All I really care about is growing out of these things." Mandy tapped one of her leg braces.

Mandy's braces were less cumbersome than they had been a year earlier, when Cindy first met her. But Cindy still couldn't see how Mandy hung on to a horse while she was wearing them or kept her balance well enough to ride on a competitive level. Cindy had always admired the younger girl's courage and tenacity. "Well, you don't really have to worry about your height or weight, since you want to jump, not flat race," she said.

"I'd better worry about everything," Mandy said. "My next show is in two weeks."

"Are you ready?" Cindy was sure Mandy would be.

"Almost, I guess." Mandy frowned. "I never think I've practiced enough."

"Yeah, I know the feeling." Cindy always wished she had more time to spend on Storm's training.

Pride's ears pricked, and he gave a quick snort. Through the colorful leaves Cindy saw Heather riding Bo around the turn in the trail.

Heather always looks a little scared on a horse, Cindy thought. *And Bo knows it*. Bo was too well trained to run off with Heather, but he couldn't seem to resist gently testing her.

"He was eating again," Heather said breathlessly as Bo approached. "I pulled his head up, though."

"That's good," Cindy said. The horses weren't supposed to eat with bridles on because the bit made it difficult for them to chew. And dried-up grass on the bridle made cleaning it a chore.

"I'm not the only one who's got a big event coming up," Mandy said. "Glory runs in the Classic in just three weeks, right?"

"If he comes out of the Jockey Club Gold Cup on Saturday okay," Cindy corrected. "The Gold Cup is a mile and a quarter, and the competition is really stiff. But we've never had soundness problems with Glory. So even if he doesn't win, no one is expecting him to get hurt and have to be scratched from the Classic."

"I know he'll win," Heather said confidently. She studied Pride for a moment. "Do you think Glory can beat Pride's time in the Classic?" Heather sounded serious.

"Of course," Cindy said quickly. Then she wondered why she was so confident—Pride had run an incredible Classic. Cindy felt disloyal thinking that way about Pride. It was the same way she had felt the night before, when Samantha talked about Shining's chances in the Breeders' Cup. *I just want so much for Glory to win,* Cindy thought. *And not just win, but break every record.*

Cindy shook her head, trying to clear away her thoughts. "Let's trot, you guys!" She squeezed her legs to cue the stallion for the faster gait. Pride didn't need to be asked twice. He immediately took off at a brisk trot. From the spring in his steps and his arched neck, Cindy knew that the stallion was enjoying himself.

"You're having fun, aren't you?" she asked. Pride's finely shaped ears flicked back as he listened to her words. *I'm having a blast, too,* Cindy thought. *I can still hardly believe I get to ride horses like Pride anytime I want. Most of the greatest jockeys in the world have never gotten to ride this guy. I'm so incredibly lucky. I should stop worrying about the Breeders' Cup and just be happy with what I have right now.*

Mandy rode on ahead again. Cindy saw that the younger girl was pointing Butterball toward a low brush jump that Samantha had set up in a clearing as part of a practice course.

Cindy pulled up Pride, and Heather stopped Bo beside them. Mandy circled Butterball, preparing for the jump. The pony's small, active hooves crunched softly in the fallen leaves.

Cindy leaned forward in the saddle, her eyes on Mandy. "I always like to watch Mandy jump," she said to Heather.

"Yeah, she's really good," Heather agreed.

Effortlessly Mandy and Butterball sailed over the jump. Cindy didn't know much about jumping form, but she could see that Mandy stayed perfectly with her mount. Already the younger girl was looking ahead to the next jump, a substantial log about five strides off.

The horses have plenty of energy, but not as much as Mandy! Cindy thought. "Just can't stop yourself from jumping, can you?" she called.

"Nope!" Mandy and Butterball soared over the log. Cindy tried to figure out whether Mandy had instructed Butterball where to take the jump or the pony had decided on his own. She couldn't tell—their partnership was virtually seamless.

Mandy and Butterball raced over four more jumps, then Mandy turned Butterball to retake the course.

"Hey, enough already!" Cindy said, laughing. She didn't think Mandy planned ever to stop.

"Okay!" But Mandy couldn't seem to resist setting Butterball at the first brush jump again. The pony hopped over it easily—he was well conditioned from Mandy's almost constant practicing.

Mandy rode over to Cindy and Heather, posting quickly to Butterball's short strides. The wind had blown her curly dark hair into disarray and she was breathing hard, but she looked happy. "I want to be sharp for the show," she said.

"You are," Cindy assured her. "Someday you have to teach me to jump like you do," she added.

"And me," Heather said wryly.

Cindy glanced at her friend with concern. Heather had been taking jumping lessons for several months now. She was improving, but Cindy knew she would never be a natural like Mandy. "You can't be the best at everything. You're the best artist in our class," Cindy reminded her friend. "You draw wonderful horses."

"Thanks." Heather smiled.

Pride pulled on the reins, as if to say that he would like to do something, too.

"I know, big guy—I'll let you out a little." Cindy looked at her friends. "I should gallop Pride," she said. "Len says he's been going stir-crazy in the barn and paddock. Poor Pride doesn't really get to run anymore. I know he misses it."

"I'll come with you," Heather said.

"I don't think Butter and I really can keep up, even though I said we could." Mandy looked ruefully at Butterball's short legs.

"I'm just going to take Pride about a mile along the lane," Cindy said. "You can catch up at the end of it."

"We won't be *very* far behind you—Butter is pretty fast." Mandy patted the pony's furry neck.

Pride clearly knew that they were going to the

galloping lane. He kept at the walk Cindy had requested but quickened his strides until he was going faster than a slow trot. Cindy bobbed up and down from the rocking gait, but she had to smile at the stallion's eagerness. She knew he wanted so much to run. Cindy didn't intend to let him all the way out, though—they'd do only a slow gallop. She couldn't risk injuring Pride, because he was a valuable freshman sire. His first crop of foals had been born the previous spring and were now promising weanlings.

"I know you've got a great new life as a sire. But you and Ashleigh must have been so disappointed when you couldn't race anymore," Cindy murmured.

She stopped Pride at the top of the galloping lane. Grassy, well-kept lanes bordered several of the paddocks at Whitebrook. Horses in training were exercised on them to increase their stamina.

Cindy waited until Heather had caught up. "Ready?" she asked. She hoped Heather was. Pride was dancing sideways, shaking his head and snorting. Cindy had her hands full trying to hold him.

"Let's go!" Heather rearranged her grip on the reins, a look of concentration on her face.

"Now, boy!" Cindy gave the stallion his head. In an instant Pride roared into a gallop. The big horse's strides were assured and smooth, eating up the ground. The white fence posts of the adjoining paddock flashed by faster than Cindy could count them.

Pride's amazing, Cindy marveled. A gust of wind shook the trees, showering Cindy and Pride with brilliantly colored leaves. Cindy laughed with sheer exuberance as she shook the leaves out of her hair. She left them in Pride's red-brown mane—the leaves were the same color and looked great.

After they had gone about a mile Cindy reluctantly increased the pressure on the reins, signaling Pride to slow. He was going too fast just for exercise.

Pride threw up his head in protest.

"Easy, big guy," Cindy said. "That's it for now. I don't want you to overdo it. You had enough of that with the Townsends." The Townsends had tried to overrace Pride, with disastrous consequences. Pride had completely lost his desire to win.

They'd better not ruin Glory's chances, Cindy thought. So far they hadn't, but Cindy's distrust of them went back a long way.

Cindy pushed her blond hair out of her face and looked around for Heather. Heather and Bo were just pounding up to them.

"That was fast!" Heather called.

"But not as fast as Glory will be on Saturday," Cindy said, feeling her heart swell with confidence and the thrill of her ride on such a wonderful day. "Glory's going to win the Jockey Club Gold Cup and then the Breeders' Cup by a mile—I've never been more sure of anything."

4

EARLY FRIDAY EVENING CINDY DODGED A CRABSTEPPING black stallion and his handler on the backside at the Belmont track and hurried toward the Whitebrook shed row. Gorgeous horses were everywhere, but Cindy hardly saw any of them. Her thoughts were only of Glory.

Just ahead of Cindy, Samantha was rushing to Shining. Cindy had flown up to Belmont with Samantha, Beth, and Ashleigh, and they had gotten off the plane less than a hour before. Cindy had finished her homework during the afternoon flight and stared longingly out the window, hoping for a tailwind. She, Samantha, and Ashleigh had driven straight to the track.

I haven't seen Glory in six weeks—what if he's forgotten me? Cindy worried as she speed-walked by a compact bay filly stubbornly tossing her head and trying to pull away from her groom. Cindy forced herself not to run—she definitely couldn't take the chance of bumping into or frightening one of these nervous, high-caliber horses. *But I wish I could fly*, she thought as she waited impatiently for a string of three horses to pass with their trainer.

At last she reached Whitebrook's shed row. "Hi, Len," Cindy said as she walked quickly down the aisle. She'd stop to catch up on news with him later, she promised herself.

"Glory's in his old stall from last summer," Len said with a smile, obviously understanding her rush.

"Hey, Len," Samantha said, going straight to Shining's stall.

"And here I thought it was me you girls had come to see," Len joked.

Cindy was too anxious to kid with Len just then. As she approached Glory's stall door she heard the quick sound of the colt's hooves as he moved around the stall.

"Glory?" Cindy called, her voice quivering with anxiety and anticipation. The sound of the big horse moving stopped.

Cindy looked into the stall. The gray colt stood frozen just inside the stall door, all four legs braced. Then, as if he could hardly believe he had heard Cindy's voice, a shiver shook his whole sleek body. He wheeled to face her.

"It's really me, boy," Cindy said, happy tears filling

her eyes. She couldn't look at him enough—from the glorious sweep of his crested, dapple gray neck to the slender elegance of his long, perfectly made legs. She reached to open the stall door so that she could see him even better.

But before she could get the door open, Glory frantically pawed it with his front hoof. Then he half reared, hopping up and down and squealing. He was almost climbing out of the stall.

"Calm down, Glory!" Cindy quickly snapped a lead line to the colt's halter and led him out into the aisle before he could hurt himself. Then she hugged him hard. Mollified now that he was near Cindy, Glory dropped his muzzle into her hair. He seemed to be trying to reassure himself that it was really her.

"He's been nervous since you left," Len acknowledged, coming up behind them. "He paces and doesn't seem to sleep as much as usual."

"Why didn't anyone tell me?" Cindy asked. If she had known, she would have found some way to convince her parents to let her come up to the track sooner.

"Well, it didn't seem to be affecting his health or training—at least not too much—so we didn't want you to worry. Right, big boy?" Len patted the colt's flank. "I walked him every morning he wasn't galloped, but a lot of the time he still wouldn't settle down."

"Oh, Glory!" Cindy leaned against the colt and closed her eyes, reveling in the nearness of her horse. She loved Storm, Wonder's Champion, and all the horses at Whitebrook, but Glory would always be first in her heart. They had been through so much together.

Cindy had helped exercise-ride and train Glory to become a racehorse, getting him over spooking, lack of focus, and other effects of the abuse he had suffered before she knew him. Glory had set a track record in his very first race. Just when Cindy had thought nothing could stop the colt, at Belmont the previous summer he had tested positive for drugs given him by a rival trainer and been disqualified from his first stakes race. But Glory had come back, winning the Brooklyn Handicap and most recently the Travers.

Cindy felt she and Glory had just survived a new kind of challenge—their separation now that he was a renowned racehorse.

Glory was shaking his head and sidestepping. He still seemed restive, Cindy thought. "When did he last get out?" she asked.

"He went for a gallop this morning with Felipe," Len said. Felipe Aragon had replaced Ashleigh as Glory's jockey and had ridden Glory to a win in the Travers. Cindy knew Felipe had a good rapport with the colt. "Glory's just excited to see you," Len added. "He'll settle down by and by."

"I'll take him out to graze. That should relax him."

Cindy ran her hand slowly over Glory's gray neck, taking in its silken softness.

"You'd better say hello to some other horses first," Len said with a laugh, reaching for Glory's lead.

Cindy realized that the barn had gotten incredibly noisy. Looking down the aisle, she saw that every horse in the Whitebrook string had popped its head out to join in the excitement. The barn rang with a chorus of whinnies and the banging of hooves on stalls.

"Okay, everybody!" Cindy said in amazement. She couldn't imagine a better welcome. First she hurried to Shining's stall. After Glory, Shining was her favorite horse.

Samantha had Shining's head in her arms. "Hi, pretty girl," Cindy said to the filly. As Shining's groom and one of the people who knew her best, Cindy couldn't help looking Shining over minutely. The roan horse's deep red coat, speckled with white, glittered like tiny rubies and diamonds. Shining was just over fifteen hands, but her muscled shoulders and hindquarters promised all the power she showed on the track.

"Isn't she perfect?" Samantha asked Cindy with a smile.

"She sure is." *But I wonder which horse is more perfect—Shining or Glory*, Cindy thought. She felt disloyal again.

Shining bobbed her beautiful head, shaking her thick black forelock as she asked for caresses.

"You're glad to see me, too, aren't you?" Cindy said softly, running her hand along Shining's red and white neck. Three weeks earlier at Belmont, Shining had come in second in the Ruffian Handicap, a grade-one race at a mile and a sixteenth, after a bad break from the gate. Shining had run a good race and almost closed to win, but she was beaten by half a length when a long-shot horse miraculously held on to the lead. Because of the effort Shining had put out, Samantha had made the decision not to race her again until the Breeders' Cup.

So what's your next race? Cindy silently asked Shining. *The Distaff or the Classic—where your competition might be Glory?* As much as Cindy might tell herself that it shouldn't matter whether Glory won or lost, she knew that it *did* matter. She wanted Glory to win more than anything.

Glory whinnied shrilly from the other end of the barn, as if to remind her that he wouldn't tolerate any more neglect.

"I can't hold this guy much longer, Cindy," Len teased. "He's about to tear down the barn."

"I'll be right there!" Cindy rushed to pet Matchless for a second. The two-year-old chestnut colt had run in a grade-two stakes at Saratoga during the summer. He had only come in third but finished gamely. In a week Ian and Mike planned to run him in an allowance race at Belmont.

43

"You're last, Mr. Wonderful, because I have to get back to Glory," Cindy said as she flew to pay Wonder's second son a moment of attention. On the small side but exquisitely made, the way Wonder's offspring always were, the honey-colored chestnut colt would run in the Champagne Stakes for two-year-olds the next day. Cindy knew that everyone at Whitebrook was watching that race almost as closely as Glory's run in the Gold Cup. The Champagne could be the first stop on the trail to the Triple Crown races for three-year-olds in the spring.

"Sammy! Cindy, sweetheart!" Ian was hurrying up the aisle, a delighted smile on his face. Ashleigh and Mike followed close behind. Cindy could feel her smile matching her dad's.

"Dad!" Samantha cried happily.

"You both look good," Ian said after he had hugged both Cindy and Samantha. "I wish I weren't away so much."

"It's okay." Cindy took Glory's lead rope again from Len. She knew there wasn't much her dad could do about his frequent absences. As a trainer, he had to be at the racetrack, wherever the horses were racing.

"I guess I'm kind of used to your being gone, Dad. This is still better than the old days," Samantha said ruefully.

Cindy remembered that when Samantha was her age, during Ian's early days as a trainer, she and her mother had moved from track to track with him. Samantha had changed schools every few months or sometimes missed school altogether for a while. A life on the road had sounded romantic to Cindy, as long as Samantha's family was all together. But after the death of Samantha's mother, the road trips had been grim. Finally Ian had accepted a job as head trainer at Whitebrook, and Samantha had found a permanent home.

Glory was restlessly pawing the concrete aisle. Clearly he was at the limit of his patience. "I'm going to take Glory out to graze," Cindy told her dad and Mike.

"Good idea." Mike nodded. "He likes to get out, and he'll stay calm with you."

On her way out Cindy looked in the stable office at Glory's monthly training chart. Every Whitebrook horse had a training chart, showing the days it had been walked, galloped, or worked and any medications it was on.

Cindy frowned as she read the abbreviations in the box for each day on Glory's chart: *W* for walk, *G* for gallop, and *WK* for work.

There're too many G's and WK's! she thought with alarm. Glory's training schedule seemed to have been compressed from his usual one—he was definitely going faster more often. The number of works worried Cindy the most. At Saratoga the previous month Glory had developed heat in one of his forelegs after too hard a work. Glory was a remarkably sound horse, but he could be hurt.

Glory snorted and pulled back on the lead line. "What's the matter, guy?" Cindy asked, tightening her grip. She heard raised voices and looked out the office door. Brad and Ashleigh were standing in front of Glory's empty stall.

"Brad, I'm not going to go over it again," Ashleigh said angrily. "Glory's not going to race this fall after the Breeders' Cup. He'll have a four-year-old season next year, you know—that is, if he lives so long at this pace!"

"We already withdrew him from the Woodward because you were afraid to run him," Brad retorted. Brad was a good-looking, dark-haired man about Ashleigh's age, but his face was twisted in an ugly sneer. He sounded just as angry as Ashleigh.

"Why would I be afraid to run Glory?" Ashleigh demanded.

"I have no idea. Probably because Princess broke down last spring in the Bluegrass," Brad said.

Cindy winced, remembering that tragic accident. Townsend Princess, Wonder's three-year-old daughter, had broken her leg in the race. Princess had endured months of pain and discomfort while her leg healed.

"But Princess has hereditary unsoundness," Brad went on. "Glory doesn't have that problem."

"How can you say that about Princess?" Ashleigh

spluttered. "Princess broke her leg the first time because she was ridden atrociously by your wife! The second break was the outcome of the first. Lavinia doesn't know the first thing about horses."

"Come on, boy." Cindy turned quickly to take Glory outside. She hated arguing. Above all, she couldn't stand to hear Princess's story again.

Suddenly Cindy saw that Lavinia was standing just inside the barn door, listening to Brad and Ashleigh. Lavinia had a strange expression on her face.

She looks like she's going to cry! Cindy thought in surprise. *Does she really care about what happened to Princess? Ashleigh doesn't think she does.* Cindy turned to warn Ashleigh that Lavinia was there, but before Cindy could open her mouth, Lavinia rushed out of the barn. Brad and Ashleigh both turned to look after her.

"This conversation isn't very productive," Brad said, glaring at Ashleigh. He hurried after Lavinia.

Ashleigh walked over to Cindy and Glory and rested her hand on the big colt's flank. "I just told him the truth," Ashleigh said with a shrug, but her voice was strained.

"I know," Cindy agreed. She didn't want Ashleigh to feel bad about defending Glory.

"Brad's right about one thing, though," Ashleigh said wearily. "I have to stop fighting with him. It's not going to change the situation."

"I don't think anybody can get along with him," Cindy said. "Except maybe Lavinia."

"Well, I have to keep trying." Ashleigh didn't look very happy.

"How can Brad think he's such a great trainer?" Cindy asked. "He almost ruined Wonder."

"He *did* ruin Wonder when he had her whipped," Ashleigh said. "But I undid the damage. Cindy, that's the lesson here—we'll just have to roll with the punches."

I don't know how we'll do that. Cindy's forehead creased with concern. Cindy thought about bringing up Glory's intense training schedule but decided not to. She was sure the stepped-up schedule was Brad's idea. If Ashleigh could have done anything about it, she would have.

"I'm going up to the racing secretary's office," Ashleigh said. "Sammy and I have to fill out some paperwork."

"Okay." Cindy looked at Glory. "And now I really am going to take you out," she said. "You've been so patient." Glory eagerly followed her to the greenest swath of grass Cindy could find.

As Cindy watched the colt reach for the grass, she wondered if the paperwork Ashleigh and Samantha were filling out had to do with Samantha's decision about running Shining in the Classic.

Maybe it doesn't even matter if Shining does run—I

48

really think Glory will win it no matter what, Cindy said to herself. *So why don't I feel good about that?*

Glory pulled strongly on the lead, half dragging Cindy to another patch of grass. "Okay, I guess this place is better," Cindy said with a laugh. "Sorry, Glory, but I'm not a great judge of grass."

Glory settled in for some serious grazing, quickly tearing off big mouthfuls. "Take your time, boy—I'm not in any hurry." Cindy sighed contentedly and tipped back her head, breathing in the familiar stable smells of horses, grain, and hay.

The evening sky was a deep purple, melting into black. Lights had gone on in the surrounding shed rows, casting pools of warm yellow illumination out the doors. Cindy could hear the calls of grooms and trainers as they organized equipment and exchanged instructions.

Near Cindy and Glory a few other grooms were grazing horses, too. Some of the horses wore colorful blankets, protection against the chill. Cindy knew Glory didn't need a blanket—he was hardly ever cold.

In the growing night the blankets faded into shades of forest green, maroon, and deep navy. Glory was a bluish, gleaming silver in the dying light. Cindy smiled, wishing Heather was there to draw the beautiful colors and horses.

Glory continued to graze the damp, cool grass. Like Cindy, he didn't seem to be in a hurry to go in.

Suddenly the colt's head shot up and his ears

pricked. Cindy stiffened. Joe Gallagher was walking straight toward them.

Cindy had no wish to talk to the trainer. The old man, with his stooped walk and gray hair, didn't look threatening, but Cindy knew that appearances could be deceiving. During the summer Joe Gallagher had almost certainly bribed a veterinary assistant and a groom to give Glory illegal drugs at the Belmont track. Glory had subsequently been disqualified from his stakes race. With Glory out of the way, Joe's best horse, Flightful, had stood a much better chance of winning at the Belmont races. After Cindy and Max had exposed Joe's scheme, Glory had come back and beaten Flightful in the Brooklyn Handicap.

Cindy knew that because of Joe's reputation, many owners, trainers, and track officials had trouble believing he had been involved in the drugging at all. Cindy was sure that he had been, though. In a way she could understand how important it was to Joe for Flightful to win. But she didn't think that excused what he had done.

"Come on, Glory." Cindy tugged lightly at Glory's lead, urging him to move to another spot. Glory reluctantly followed her a step, then dropped his head and resumed grazing.

To her relief, Cindy saw Len emerging from the Whitebrook shed row. She realized he must have been watching them.

Len intercepted Joe before he could approach Cindy, and the trainer and stable manager exchanged words. "What could they be talking about?" Cindy murmured to Glory. "Nobody at Whitebrook has anything to say to Joe Gallagher."

Glory continued blissfully cropping grass. He seemed to be saying, *No one's going to distract me from my treat.*

Joe disappeared into the shed row where his horses were stabled, and Cindy breathed a sigh of relief. Next time she would find somewhere else for Glory to graze. Len walked over to join them.

"How come you talked to him?" Cindy asked.

"I think it's better to speak to him and find out what's on his mind," Len said.

"So is Joe still after Glory?" *Not that he would admit it if he was*, she thought.

"I don't think so." Len looked thoughtful. "Joe said he's going to retire from training after this year. He's getting old, and his health isn't good."

"I'll be glad when he isn't around."

Len hesitated. "Joe seems sorry about that trouble last summer."

"*Now* he's sorry." Cindy didn't believe it.

"I'll still keep an eye on him," Len said. "But I think we're past all that. Why don't you bring Glory in now and we'll feed him?"

Inside the barn Ashleigh had just finished giving

51

the other horses their evening ration of grain, vitamins, and minerals. Cindy put Glory in his stall and went to the feed room to scoop his grain into a bucket. When she poured out the feed for the colt, he immediately plunged his nose deep into it and munched.

"So tomorrow the Gold Cup for Glory, in three weeks the Classic," Ashleigh said. "Maybe I'm imagining it, but he seems a lot happier since you got here."

Cindy smiled. "Thanks—I think he is." Cindy knew that she was certainly much happier now that she and Glory were together again. "Do you think Glory will win tomorrow?" she asked.

"He's going up against stiff competition, but it's nothing he can't handle," Ashleigh said. "Flightful will probably give Glory a run for his money—he has a couple of times. It's always guesswork how a race will play out, though. Wow, I think I'm going to sit down and rest my feet. Being pregnant means I'm tired sometimes."

"Do you know yet if the baby's a boy or a girl?" Cindy asked as Ashleigh sat carefully on a hay bale.

"No. The doctor is pretty sure he knows from the sonograms, but I asked him not to tell me. Speaking of imagining things, my intuition tells me the baby's a girl. Don't hold me to that, though." Ashleigh smiled.

"A girl would be nice," Cindy said. Whatever its

sex, she was sure that with Ashleigh and Mike for parents, the baby would be up on a horse before its first birthday.

"Anyway, Glory certainly doesn't have the Gold Cup in the bag, but I'm more interested in how the Breeders' Cup race will go." Ashleigh looked thoughtful. "I wonder if Glory's run in the Classic will be a real fight, the way Pride's was. His race was neck and neck the whole way. Wonder was competing in her Classic against Townsend Prince, her half-brother, but the outcome was in doubt for only a few seconds—Wonder ran a perfect race."

"What do you think Glory's competition in the Classic will be like?" Cindy asked. She hoped that Ashleigh would tell her what Samantha had decided about Shining.

"So far it's shaping up to be an excellent field. I'm not too worried about any of the European horses—they're usually more of a threat on turf. But Treasure's Prospect, the champion three-year-old from Florida, will almost certainly be running, and so will Chance Remark, who won the Belmont this year. And then there's Flightful. He really pounded the competition on the West Coast this summer."

Cindy thought a moment. Glory would have two kinds of competition in the Classic—against Flightful and the rest of the field, and against Wonder, Pride, and all the other champion horses that had previously won the most prestigious race in the world. *I want him to win against all of them,* she said to herself fiercely.

"And maybe Shining will run in the Classic," Ashleigh said softly.

"Samantha still hasn't decided?" Cindy asked, feeling a crawling sense of dread.

"No—haven't you talked to her about it? Shining's entered in both the Classic and the Distaff right now. But my sense is that Samantha's leaning toward the Classic."

"Sammy didn't say anything to me about it. When does she have to decide?" Cindy asked.

"Not until about a week before the race. So she has another two weeks to think it over."

Cindy leaned over Glory's stall door to watch her horse. He was still eating contentedly, occasionally flicking an ear in her direction. *I wish Shining didn't have to run in the Classic,* Cindy thought. *No matter who wins, somebody is going to feel terrible.*

5

"HOW DO YOU THINK KELLY MORGAN WILL DO ON MR. Wonderful?" Cindy asked, leaning around Beth in the grandstand to talk to Ashleigh. The young jockey had just ridden Mr. Wonderful onto the track for the post parade, along with the rest of the ten-horse field for the grade-one Champagne Stakes. Ian, Mike, Ashleigh, and Samantha were all studying the field through binoculars.

"Kelly really hit it off with Mr. Wonderful," Ashleigh said. "I know you must think that's impossible after her disastrous rides on Glory last summer. But Mr. Wonderful is an entirely different horse."

That's true, Cindy thought. Kelly hadn't been able to hold on to Glory or keep his attention on the track. As a result, Glory had lost the Jim Dandy and almost lost his chance to run in the Breeders' Cup. Cindy was glad

Felipe Aragon would be riding Glory that afternoon in the Gold Cup. Sensitive but firm, Felipe had a much better rapport with Glory.

Mr. Wonderful's behavior was in striking contrast to that of some of the other two-year-olds in the race, Cindy thought. Splendiferous, a dapple gray like Glory, whinnied shrilly and leaped across the track, pulling away from the escort rider. His jockey quickly circled the colt until the escort rider could grasp his bridle again. Because the horses in this race were all just two years old, Cindy knew that frisky behavior could be expected.

Mr. Wonderful was walking quietly clockwise on the track, occasionally stopping to look around. The warm Indian-summer sunlight turned his chestnut coat and his flowing mane and tail to a brilliant gold.

"He's the most beautiful horse out there," Beth observed.

"He really is," Samantha said. "All Wonder's offspring are gorgeous, but he's show quality. And he couldn't be better conditioned." She looked over at Ashleigh. "Don't you think?"

"I just hope Mr. Wonderful makes it through the race," Ashleigh said grimly.

"Why?" Cindy was startled. She hadn't realized Ashleigh was anticipating trouble.

"Oh, Brad and I argued endlessly about Mr. Wonderful's training, too, when we had Mr. Wonderful in Kentucky." Ashleigh shook her head.

"At least you were there to keep an eye on him," Mike said.

"Yes," Ashleigh agreed. "And he does look magnificent."

Cindy couldn't agree more. She was sure Mr. Wonderful's race would go well. After all, Ashleigh had stayed at Whitebrook for most of the fall so that she could closely supervise every minute of Mr. Wonderful's training. And her hard work had already paid off—Mr. Wonderful had won an allowance race at Turfway Park in September. He had been vanned to Belmont the previous week.

"This is Mr. Wonderful's last race of the year." Ashleigh leaned forward as she studied the field. "I want to bring him along slowly. He's technically a two-year-old, but he was born in May, so he's young for two." Cindy knew that all Thoroughbreds turned a year older on January first, regardless of the date of their actual birthday.

"I bet that doesn't suit Brad," Samantha commented.

"Not at all—he wants to campaign Mr. Wonderful this winter." Ashleigh frowned. "Brad may be right that I'm being too cautious with Mr. Wonderful's training. His barb about the unsoundness in Wonder's line did strike home. I really am afraid for Mr. Wonderful after what happened to Wonder, Pride, and Princess."

Cindy didn't know what to say. She had no idea

how Ashleigh could stop Brad's interference with the horses' training.

The horses approached the starting gate. Cindy could see that some of the two-year-olds didn't like the look of the large, metallic contraption. Too Much Chatter, a smallish bay and the first to be loaded, had frozen in front of the gate, planting his hooves. Attendants pulled on his bridle and the colt reared, spilling the attendants right and left. The jockey gripped Too Much Chatter's mane and kept his seat.

"If that horse doesn't go in the gate in a minute, I bet he's going on the gate list," Samantha remarked.

"What's that?" Cindy asked. Glory had always had excellent gate manners—she didn't know what happened to horses that didn't.

"Before any horse can race, it has to demonstrate for track officials that it can satisfactorily break from a gate," Ian said. "The situation would be too dangerous otherwise. The horse could flip over and crush the jockey or interfere with other horses coming out of the gate."

"After that kind of thing, a horse can't race again until it demonstrates to track officials that it can behave itself in the gate," Samantha continued.

Too Much Chatter suddenly popped into the gate. He seemed almost to have sensed that he was about to be thrown out of the race—or his jockey did and gave the colt extra urging, Cindy thought. She felt proud as Mr. Wonderful quietly loaded into the four position.

He had always been an almost perfect horse to train and ride.

The track was silent for an instant after the last horse loaded. Then the gates crashed open, the bell ringing shrilly. The track exploded with the sound of thundering hooves, dust, and the roar of the crowd.

Mr. Wonderful broke sharply from the gate. In an instant Kelly had angled him into a good position along the rail, just off the two front-runners, Splendiferous and Bright of Morning, a light gray colt.

"Perfect position!" Ashleigh was sitting on the edge of her seat. Cindy knew how much this race meant to her. If Mr. Wonderful won, he would be on his way to the Kentucky Derby.

The horses maintained their positions going into the backstretch. Then Mr. Wonderful began to inch up on Bright of Morning. The gray colt fought back furiously, but in a few strides Mr. Wonderful had put him away. The horses pounded around the far turn into the stretch.

"And they're headed for home!" the announcer called. "It's still Splendiferous on the lead, with Mr. Wonderful two lengths back. Four lengths back to Bright of Morning . . . "

Cindy stared intently at the track. Kelly was fully crouched over Mr. Wonderful's neck, urgently requesting speed to go after Splendiferous. But Mr. Wonderful wasn't responding! The chestnut colt was trying to hold on, but Splendiferous increased his lead

59

to three lengths. At Mr. Wonderful's flank Too Much Chatter was closing fast. The horses flashed by the eighth pole.

"Make your move, Mr. Wonderful!" Cindy cried. "You're running out of time!"

"Kelly's asking Mr. Wonderful for more, but he doesn't have it." Samantha buried her hands in her hair.

"Yes, he does," Ashleigh cried. "Look!"

Cindy could hardly believe it. Mr. Wonderful had changed leads and found another gear. At that instant the sun emerged from behind a cloud, suffusing the track with a clear yellow light. A sunburst of gold himself, Mr. Wonderful roared up on Splendiferous. He was a length behind, then a neck. Seconds later the horses were a nose apart, and the wire was looming!

Cindy was on her feet with the rest of the crowd. "Go, boy," she screamed. "Take charge—you can do it!"

As if he had heard her, Mr. Wonderful dug in to take a huge stride. The colts flashed across the finish— and Mr. Wonderful was out in front!

"Mr. Wonderful wins it by a neck and driving," the announcer called.

"I can hardly believe it." Ashleigh's hazel eyes sparkled with delight. "I think you're looking at Whitebrook's next Derby contender, everybody!"

I'm looking at the most beautiful horse in the world, except for Glory, Cindy thought, smiling broadly as she followed Ashleigh to the winner's circle. *I know I won't ever forget how Mr. Wonderful looked in that race.*

"Here we go, big guy." Len rested a steadying hand on Glory's shoulder that afternoon as he and Cindy led the big colt around the walking ring with Felipe Aragon up in the saddle. In just half an hour the Jockey Club Gold Cup would go off.

Cindy looked out into the crowd, seeing hundreds of excited, happy faces mobbing the saddling paddock. Crowds always gathered to look over the horses before the race, almost like at a horse show.

This is a show, Cindy thought proudly, *of the fastest Thoroughbreds!*

"There's March to Glory!" called a teenage girl. "He's even more gorgeous than he looks on TV."

"He sure is!" answered a tall blond woman.

Cindy knew they were right. The powerful gray colt was lightly high-stepping, showing off his sleek, muscled body, yet he was completely under control. From his glossy dappled neck to his flowing black and gray tail, Glory was the perfect image of breeding, power, and beauty.

Ian met Felipe and Glory coming out of the walking ring. "There are some real contenders in the race, but nothing Glory can't handle," Ian said to Felipe. "I'd take him straight to the front and keep him there. Whatever you do, don't get caught in crowd problems.

Flightful, Unbridled Energy, and Beyond Price all like to go right to the front, so you'll have to beat them out for position."

Glory snorted and looked eagerly after the first horses in the field, who were already walking toward the tunnel leading to the track. "You want to go with them, don't you?" Cindy whispered, filled with love for her horse. The big colt gleamed a soft silver in the hazy gray afternoon light. "The sky's the color of your coat," she told him. "Just like the sun was the color of Mr. Wonderful's. I think that's a good sign."

"Sign or no sign, Glory's got plenty of confidence, and so do I," Felipe said. The wiry, dark-haired jockey reached down to stroke Glory's neck. "Maybe by now I've got this big guy's number." Felipe laughed. "All I have to worry about is what everyone else is doing in the race."

Just behind Glory, Cindy saw Flightful coming up with Joe Gallagher. The stocky black horse, with his Roman nose and thick neck, would never win a beauty contest, Cindy thought. But the other colt's bunchy, rippling muscles and energetic stride belied first impressions. *He's going to be a real contender in the Gold Cup,* Cindy realized.

"See you later, Glory," she said softly. "I wish I could go out there with you. But in a way I can—I'll be thinking about you every minute of the race!"

Glory tossed his head, as if he appreciated the

support. Then the big colt stood very still, his muzzle touching Cindy's hands. For a minute it seemed to Cindy that Glory hardly noticed the hubbub of horses, jockeys, owners, trainers, and the eager, pushing crowd as he quietly breathed in her scent. Then he lifted his muzzle and looked toward the track again.

"Right—it's time to go," Cindy said. "Good luck, Felipe!"

"Thanks." Felipe touched his crop to his helmet, then pointed Glory toward the track.

Cindy rushed to the stands so that she wouldn't miss a minute of the post parade. *I can tell a lot about Glory's chances just by watching his mood on the track*, she thought.

"Cindy! Up here!" Samantha waved from their seats in the grandstand.

Cindy climbed the stairs and sat between Samantha and Ashleigh. Cindy always liked to hear their perceptive analysis of races—especially Glory's.

"The Gold Cup is interesting this year," Samantha commented. "Both Glory and Flightful, the two favorites, are colts who have come from behind."

"Flightful has done so well this summer at the California tracks, he'll almost certainly run in the Classic," Ian said.

"We'll see about Shining," Samantha said quietly.

Ian nodded. "You know her best—at this point I'll leave it up to you."

Cindy gulped. She wished Samantha would make up her mind one way or the other. The suspense was killing her. Cindy turned her attention back to the track.

"Why is Glory being ponied to the gate?" she asked in surprise. She knew that most racehorses were calmer when they were accompanied to the gate by another horse. But Glory had never needed one.

Ashleigh shrugged. "I didn't ask for an escort rider. I guess it's one of Brad's ideas. But I don't think it can hurt."

Just then Glory jumped and shied away from the pony. For a terrible moment Cindy thought the colt would run into Unbridled Energy, who was trotting nearby, or even go out of control on the track.

Ponying Glory is another one of Brad's bad ideas, Cindy thought, feeling her muscles tense.

Felipe tightened up on Glory's reins and seemed to say a few soothing words to him. In moments he had the colt stepping along smoothly again, following the pony.

Glory loaded well into the gate after Flightful, the number-one horse. Glory had drawn the two position.

"Here we go," Beth said as the last horse walked into the gate. She reached across Samantha and squeezed Cindy's hand.

Please win it, Glory! Cindy willed the colt silently. *Set another record!*

"And they're off!" the announcer shouted. At the break Glory and Flightful both leaped into the lead, churning up clumps of dirt and almost jostling as they fought for position. For the first quarter mile the two horses were so close, Cindy couldn't tell which was ahead. "Are they going to have a speed duel?" she asked her dad fearfully. If Glory and Flightful pushed the pace too much, they could both burn out.

"I don't know, but if they do, Flightful will be the loser." Ian was looking intently through his binoculars. "Flightful's made an impression on the West Coast, but I don't think he's a match for Glory."

As if he had heard Ian's words, Glory suddenly put on a burst of speed. The big gray colt put his nose ahead of Flightful's as they whipped across the backstretch.

"Glory has such lovely action," Ashleigh said.

Cindy nodded, but she saw a new problem emerging. Unbridled Energy and Beyond Price were coming up on the inside along the rail. Flightful must be drifting out a little and leaving them room, Cindy realized. But it didn't look like enough for them to get by.

That's not good! Cindy barely had time to think before Beyond Price skimmed the rail and bore out, bumping Unbridled Energy. Cindy watched in horror as the horses running almost abreast hit each other like dominoes.

Flightful bumped Glory! Glory staggered, nearly unseating Felipe. Cindy knew how dangerous Glory's imbalance could be. Thousands of pounds of force hammered each of Glory's legs with each stride. If his stride was jagged, even more stress would be applied to his legs.

Felipe managed to hang on. He must have seen the other horses coming sideways across the track and prepared himself for the impact, Cindy realized. Still off balance, Unbridled Energy and Beyond Price bumped again. Beyond Price went down, throwing his jockey into the infield.

"No, this is terrible!" Cindy cried. A moment later she saw that the situation was even worse than she had thought. Beyond Price, the fallen jockey's horse, was running riderless down the track, right in Glory's path. Glory veered around him, recovered his stride, and gamely plunged on. But Flightful's trip had been the least troubled by the collision, and he was in the lead by four lengths!

The horses roared into the far turn. Glory was bounding after Flightful, but the black horse was moving extremely quickly. *I don't know if Glory can close!* Cindy thought. She felt on the verge of tears from the bad luck and disappointment. She did notice that Glory and Flightful were running so fast, they were ahead of the riderless horse. That was amazing in itself, since that horse had so much less weight to carry.

"Thank goodness the interference didn't knock

Glory out of the race," Beth said. "And the jockey is getting up—he wasn't hurt."

"That's what I call a traffic problem," Mike said anxiously.

"Did the other jockeys push Glory on purpose to stop him?" Cindy asked hoarsely. "Flightful—"

"Not possible!" Ashleigh called over the noise of the crowd. "Blocking another horse is one thing, but deliberately ramming it is too dangerous. The jockey bumping the other horse and his own mount could be badly injured."

Biting her knuckle, Cindy watched Glory, praying she wouldn't discover that he had hurt his legs in the collision. To her relief, his strides seemed strong and even. But she didn't think he could catch Flightful. The black colt was holding on, and he didn't seem to be laboring.

Suddenly Glory's ears swept back close to his head. Cindy jumped up, her heart in her throat. "He's going to run a Just Victory race!" she cried.

"What?" Mike looked puzzled. But Samantha nodded, not taking her eyes off the track.

Cindy was sure that Glory knew he needed to run what she called a Just Victory race—a race like so many that Just Victory, his famous grandsire, had run, in which courage and sheer will to win would decide the outcome. Glory resembled Just Victory in looks and in his phenomenal speed and heart.

The magnificent gray colt began to draw off. "And March to Glory is launching his winning bid," the announcer called.

"Felipe has enough horse left!" Mike said tensely. Glory was just off the front-runner heading into the stretch.

"March to Glory has found his best stride," the announcer shouted.

"Yes, Glory!" Cindy screamed. "Yes, oh, yes!"

"There's no stopping him!" Samantha's face wore an expression of pure delight. Glory blazed under the wire, still increasing his speed.

"And March to Glory wins it by a length after a troubled trip," the announcer called.

"He showed true class," Ashleigh said with conviction.

"He did!" Cindy couldn't stop smiling. She could hardly believe the effort Glory had put in. She turned to leave the stands, wishing the people in front of her would move faster. She wanted to get to the winner's circle and tell Glory just how well he had done.

"I don't think there's any question where we're going next with Glory." Ian smiled at Cindy.

Cindy took a deep breath. "To the Breeders' Cup!" she said with a grin.

6

"DON'T WORRY, BABY," CINDY SOOTHED THREE DAYS LATER as she led Wonder's Champion away from Wonder for the very first time. Len had returned to Whitebrook from Belmont ahead of Cindy, but she had asked Len to wait to wean the colt until she got back from the track. Cindy felt that weaning him was something she should do. Samantha, Ashleigh, and Mike had returned home with her, and they were all expert horsepeople, but Wonder's Champion had always been Cindy's special favorite.

The dark chestnut foal followed her easily out of the paddock. Cindy had led him around the paddock since the day after he was born. But Cindy doubted he would keep coming this easily—he just didn't know yet what was going on.

"I promise it's going to be okay," Cindy went on, shutting the gate behind them. She thought the sound

69

of her familiar voice might reassure the foal during this difficult time. "We've known each other since the day you were born—I wouldn't lie to you."

Suddenly Wonder's Champion didn't seem to believe her. He balked, digging in all four small hooves, and whinnied shrilly for his mother.

"I know, little fellow," Len said, coming up on the colt's right side and deftly attaching another lead line to move him along. "But this has got to be done."

Cindy was glad of Len's assistance. Wonder's Champion was still small, but only compared to a grown horse. Sturdy, muscular, and extremely stubborn, he was the last foal of that year's crop to be weaned. Since he had been born in May, very late in the year, Ashleigh had wanted to give him a little more time with Wonder. But now, with winter fast approaching, Cindy knew it was time to give Wonder a rest and for Wonder's Champion to be on his own.

The young horse didn't understand why he had to leave his mother, though. Cindy's heart wrenched as Wonder's Champion whinnied piercingly, his entire small body shaking. Because she and the foal were so close, Cindy had hoped her presence would make weaning easier on him.

Right now nothing seems to be helping much, she thought. *But at least he's following me away from Wonder.*

Wonder was frantically running around the pasture where Vic Teleski, one of Whitebrook's full-time

70

grooms and exercise riders, had just released her. Wonder was whinnying loudly. "She's just as upset as he is," Cindy said. She knew she sounded upset herself. It was hard for her to bear seeing the mare in so much pain.

Len nodded. "Even though she's had three other foals, this is still hard."

With halting steps Cindy and Len managed to pull Wonder's Champion to the back paddock. Cindy opened the gate and quickly released him.

The six young horses already in the paddock had been weaned weeks ago and were calmly grazing. "You'll have lots of company here," she told him.

Wonder's Champion stood stock still, staring at the other weanlings.

"He can't understand why they aren't upset," Cindy said to Len.

"He will, though," Len said reassuringly.

Cindy opened the gate and walked over to Wonder's Champion. The colt looked at her, then gave a small, unhappy whinny.

"Hush," Cindy said, reaching to stroke his neck. For the first time in his life the colt backed away from her gentle touch. His small, compact body was rigid with fear, and his ears were pricked, listening for Wonder.

"I know, boy—I'm so sorry it hurts," Cindy said softly. "But you're going to be all right."

The colt ignored her. He stood frozen, silent. Cindy

knew the baby still expected, or maybe just hoped by now, to hear his mother's voice.

"You're not all alone," Cindy went on. "I'm here. I'll always be here."

Wonder's Champion looked up at her, pain in his beautiful dark eyes. With a last little whinny, he took an exploratory step toward Cindy.

Cindy was surprised. She had never seen a young horse accept comfort from a person right after weaning. In her experience weanlings had to spend at least a couple of hours getting over the shock of separation before they were willing to socialize again.

The other weanlings in the paddock were still cropping grass, ignoring Wonder's Champion. *Maybe since he was weaned alone, he's turning to me instead of them*, she thought. *How incredible—it's almost like I'm another horse.*

The colt touched his muzzle to her hands. Cindy lifted one hand slowly to try to stroke him again. This time the colt permitted it. Cindy ran her hand down his deep brown neck and finally hugged him. "Now you're going to be okay," she murmured.

Wonder's Champion looked at Cindy for a long moment. His big eyes seemed to hold a question.

"Yes, I know," she said softly. "You and I are going to be very special to each other."

"You really have a way with horses." Len shook his head admiringly. "I've known that since the first day I saw you with those orphan foals, Rainbow and Four Leaf Clover."

Cindy stayed with Wonder's Champion until the colt had relaxed enough to start grazing. A few of the other young horses in the paddock wandered over and sniffed the newcomer curiously. Limitless Time, a small bay colt and the son of Ashleigh's star race mare Fleet Goddess, sprang a few steps off and looked back to see if Wonder's Champion wanted to play.

"Go ahead," Cindy urged him.

Wonder's Champion hesitated, then trotted after the other weanling. Cindy let herself out the gate. When she looked back, Wonder's Champion had stopped to watch her.

"It's okay!" she called, smiling. "Have fun with your buddy!"

Wonder's Champion turned to the other colt. When Cindy looked back again, the two weanlings were playing a spirited game of chase around the paddock.

He'll be fine now, Cindy thought as she walked quickly up to the barn to get Storm for his training session. Samantha had picked her up early at school that day so that Cindy would have more time to help with Wonder's Champion, but night was fast approaching. Cindy knew she had to hurry or she wouldn't have any time with Storm at all.

In the barn Len had crosstied the dark gray colt and was brushing him. Cindy had to smile when she saw how relaxed Storm was. The colt stood on three legs, with his eyes half closed and his head hanging. When he saw her, he opened his eyes wide and pricked his ears, as if to say, *Now I'll see some action!*

"I've just about got him ready," Len said.

"Thanks, Len," Cindy said gratefully. Without Len's help, she would have had even less time to train the colt, since she never skimped on his grooming or other care. "Where's Storm's saddle pad?" Cindy asked, looking around the clean, roomy barn. She had set Storm's saddle, bridle, and saddle pad on his stall door right after school.

"In the wash," Len said.

"I'll just borrow somebody else's." Cindy walked to the tack room. *I'll grab one of Glory's,* she thought. Usually she didn't use one horse's brushes or tack on another, in order to minimize the chance of transmitting skin diseases. But Glory's saddle pads hadn't been used for months.

In the dim tack room, rows of polished saddles hung on posts set in the wall. Glory's post, with his name on a brass plate, was empty except for an old saddle pad.

Imp was sitting on it. "Sorry, guy, but you have to move," Cindy said.

As if he understood her words, the cat yawned, stretched, and leaped to the floor. Cindy pulled down the saddle pad. It had a few tears and wasn't considered good enough to take to the track anymore. All Glory's new pads were at the track with him.

Cindy touched the saddle pad to her cheek, breathing in Glory's faint scent. She tried to chase away a deep feeling of loneliness. *After the Breeders' Cup, Glory will be home for the winter*, she reminded herself. *We'll have plenty of time to be together then.* Ian, Mike, and Ashleigh had all been firm that Glory would get a rest until spring even if he won the Classic. Absently Cindy rubbed the saddle pad against her cheek, imagining trail rides with Glory at Christmas through fresh, powdery snow.

Storm snorted loudly from the aisle. With a start Cindy realized she'd been daydreaming—and keeping the colt waiting.

"I'm sorry, boy," she apologized, hurrying back to him. "We'll get going."

Cindy noticed that Imp was following her. "You wonder where I'm going with Glory's saddle pad, don't you?" she asked the cat.

Imp twined around her feet adoringly. Cindy smoothed the saddle pad on Storm's back and turned to pick up the saddle.

With an amazingly high leap, Imp jumped up on the pad. He barely made it to the side of the pad, then scrabbled his way to the top. Storm spooked at the sudden impact of the cat's weight, bracing his legs. He twisted his head to try to see what was on his back.

Cindy took a quick step to Storm's side, ready to release him from the crossties immediately if he became any more frightened. He could injure his head or neck pulling against the ties in a panic.

Undeterred by his unfriendly reception, Imp stalked up and down Storm's back and purred. The colt's ears went back to a relaxed position. Obviously he had decided to accept the cat as well.

"So, Imp, you finally think Storm is okay?" Cindy asked with a laugh. "You've each got a new gray friend."

Removing the cat, Cindy saddled up Storm. The young horse stood quietly, as if being tacked up was old hat to him now, Cindy noted with satisfaction.

"I'll come out with you," Len said, walking over from the stable office. Cindy had expected that Len would accompany them, as he always did. Storm was a gentle colt, but Cindy knew that a young horse could be unpredictable. She never exercised him alone.

As she led Storm to the yearling ring, Cindy sniffed the pungent, tangy smell of wood smoke coming from Ashleigh and Mike's beautiful farmhouse. The day was cold and overcast, and a faint drizzle formed a fine mist on Storm's dark gray coat. Cindy didn't mind the weather as long as Storm didn't slip. *I wonder if I like gray days more now that I've got two gray horses*, she thought contentedly.

In the ring Cindy mounted the colt and put him through his warm-ups at a walk and trot. The rain began to come down a little harder, turning Storm's charcoal gray neck and flanks almost black. Cindy pushed her damp hair out of her face and looked at Len for instructions.

"Let's work on his right lead today," Len said. "He doesn't go as well on that one."

Cindy nodded and gathered her reins. She knew that most horses, including Storm, were "left-handed"—they preferred to gallop on the left lead. But racehorses had to go on both leads equally well. Especially in the stretch, a horse could get an extra kick by changing leads to rest the leg that had been leading.

"Be careful, Cindy," Len said. "It's getting slippery out here."

"I will, but maybe this is good for Storm. He has to learn to handle mud." The rain had soaked the top of Cindy's head and was beginning to run into her eyes, but she wiped it away and prepared to continue Storm's training session. She remembered that two of Glory's races had been run on muddy tracks. Part of what made Glory a superhorse, Cindy thought, was that he could handle any track surface—and win on it. Cindy had helped him to get that way by riding him on the trails through mud and exercising him no matter what the weather. Cindy was determined to do the same for Storm.

The colt obediently picked up the right lead as Cindy pulled his head to the outside and clucked to him, but Cindy could feel that Storm wasn't nearly as balanced on the right lead as he was on the left. His strides were a little choppy, and he seemed to want to change back to the left lead. Storm began to cross-canter, an awkward, difficult-to-sit gait in which the colt was half on one lead with his front legs and half on the other lead with his back legs.

Cindy pulled the colt's head firmly to the outside, trying to get him out of the cross canter. At that instant she felt the colt's balance begin to go completely.

He's going to fall! Desperately Cindy shifted her weight left, away from the direction of the fall, and tightened up on the reins, trying to help Storm stay upright. For just a second Cindy had a vision of the crushing impact the colt's thousand-pound weight would have on her leg if he fell to the ground on her.

With a jerk of his legs, twisting his entire body, Storm regained his balance and cantered on. The gait was uneven, although not a cross canter, and Cindy could feel how tight his muscles were from his scare. She was frightened, too, and her hands were trembling. Cindy pulled the colt down to a walk.

"Let's stop for today," Len called. "That was a close one." Cindy heard the concern in his voice.

"Just one more time around on the right lead." Cindy drew a deep breath and reached forward to pat Storm's wet neck. "We've got to get you going well on your right lead for your stretch drive," she told the colt. "I think yours is going to be very fast."

7

IT'S SO GREAT BEING IN CHARGE AT THE FARM, CINDY thought happily as she walked up the path to the mares' barn the next Saturday. The day was cool, and the air smelled fresh and sweet from the rainstorm that had ended earlier that morning. The previous night Beth had flown in from Belmont, and she, along with Samantha, Ashleigh, and Mike, had gone for Saturday brunch at nearby Oakridge Meadows, a large breeding farm. Len and Vic were repairing the back paddock fence, and Cindy was looking after the horses.

Cindy was enjoying her new responsibilities, but she intended to be careful about them as well. She had already checked on the stallions. Pride was in the back paddock, contentedly cropping grass. The rest of the stallions—Jazzman, Maxwell, Blues King, and Sadler's Station—were in their spacious stalls. The stallions were rotated into the paddock from their stalls, because they had to be put out to graze alone.

Cindy stepped into the roomy, dimly lit mares' barn. All the mares and fillies except Townsend Princess were out in the paddock. Ever since Princess had broken her leg, only Ashleigh could safely take her out to graze.

Princess put her exquisitely sculpted head over her stall door. She bobbed her head, asking for attention.

"I'm coming, girl," Cindy reassured her. As always, her heart ached at the sight of the injured filly. Cindy approached Princess slowly and cautiously, trying not to startle her. Princess's broken leg had mended, but it would always be weak. Even a sudden misstep might cause her to break it again.

Princess seemed to know. She stood perfectly still, looking like a statue of the perfect Thoroughbred. *Except for her broken leg, she is perfect,* Cindy thought sadly.

"I'm sorry, girl," Cindy said, rubbing the filly's forehead. "If there were some way to make it up to you, I would." Princess whickered softly, as if to say that she was satisfied with Cindy's visit.

"How is that horse doing?"

Cindy forced herself not to jump at the sound of Lavinia Townsend's loud voice. Princess stirred uneasily.

"Pretty well." Cindy quickly moved away from Princess. Cindy's heart was hammering. She prayed

Lavinia wouldn't approach Princess and upset her somehow.

"Where's Mr. Wonderful?" Brad asked, coming up beside his wife.

"Out in the paddock," Cindy answered politely. Mr. Wonderful had returned from Belmont a few days earlier, and except for a light gallop the day before, Ashleigh had taken him out of training. *Now what?* she wondered.

"Would you please go get Mr. Wonderful and tack him up?" Lavinia asked.

Her request sounded like an order. With a sinking feeling, Cindy noticed that Brad and Lavinia were both wearing breeches and riding boots. *They're going to ride him*, she realized. *But Ashleigh wanted him to rest!*

Cindy walked slowly out of the barn, catching up a lead rope as she went. She had to do what they said— she had no choice. Brad was Mr. Wonderful's half owner, and if she didn't go get him, Brad would.

Mr. Wonderful was grazing peacefully in one of the paddocks. He lifted his head and looked at her, seeming mildly surprised to see her again so soon. Cindy had just put him out.

"Come on, boy," Cindy said, clipping the lead rope to his halter. "We have to do what they want. If I had a bridle, I think I might gallop you away from them. Why do adults think they have the right to just push me around?"

81

Mr. Wonderful nudged her as if he sympathized. Cindy fed him a carrot, breaking it into little bits so it would take as long as possible. With a heavy sigh she finally led him up to the barn.

"How long was he out?" Brad asked as Cindy crosstied the colt in the aisle.

"Only about ten minutes." Cindy hated to tell the truth. Since Mr. Wonderful hadn't had time to eat much, he could be ridden.

"Good—he can be breezed."

Breezed? Cindy stared at Brad in astonishment. "But Mr. Wonderful is off for the winter." Cindy knew that the colt had strained a tendon in the spring, and Ashleigh didn't want to push him. And Brad almost always rode hard.

"I'm taking him out of retirement right now," Brad said dryly. "Tack him up, and let's get going."

Cindy felt sick as she brushed Mr. Wonderful's silken coat. *Isn't it enough that Brad sticks his nose in Glory's training all the time?* she thought. *Does he have to show up here, too?*

Silently Cindy tacked up Mr. Wonderful. She knew that Ashleigh would be furious that Brad was going behind her back. Cindy only hoped Ashleigh wouldn't be furious with her, too, for not thinking of a way to prevent this.

"Okay, let's go." Brad took the colt's reins.

Cindy followed them to the oval, still trying to

think how she could talk Brad out of riding. Len and Vic were far away in the back paddock, bent over the fence they were repairing.

They're too far away to help! she thought desperately. *I can't leave Mr. Wonderful to run and get them, either.*

Brad stopped the colt at the gap. "You ride him," he said in a clipped voice, handing Cindy the reins.

"But I can't!" Cindy stared at Brad in horror. She had only ridden Mr. Wonderful once, at a slow gallop. *What if I ride him wrong and injure him again?*

Brad yanked the reins out of her hand. "I haven't got all day. I'll ride him."

"No, I will." Cindy's mind was racing. She couldn't let Brad touch the colt. Mr. Wonderful would probably get a better ride from her, even if it wasn't a good one.

She tried to warm the colt up slowly at a walk and a trot, then eased him into a gallop. Mr. Wonderful responded well to her signals. *So far, so good*, she thought. They rounded the far turn.

"Take him around one more time, then breeze him a quarter mile," Brad called as Cindy rode by the gap.

"That's too much for him—I shouldn't!" Cindy circled Mr. Wonderful to bring him to a stop in front of them.

Lavinia sighed. "Cindy, don't be afraid. But then, you probably *are* too young to be on a spirited horse like that."

Cindy tightened her grip on the reins, then relaxed

it, trying not to communicate her anger to the horse. A horrible thought crossed her mind—was Lavinia thinking about riding Mr. Wonderful? *Ashleigh would never forgive me if I let that happen*, Cindy said to herself. *I just have to ride the way they want me to.*

"Speed up the gallop," Brad ordered. "You're going too slow to warm him up for the breeze."

"I don't want to take him faster!" Cindy cried.

"Get off the horse," Brad said impatiently. "I'll ride him."

Cindy dismounted. Before she could protest, Brad had ridden off.

Cindy closed her eyes, willing Mr. Wonderful to be okay. But when she looked out at the track, Brad was pounding the colt across the backstretch, and with every stride they were going faster. *He'd never dare to ride him like that if anyone else was around*, Cindy thought, feeling close to tears.

Brad trotted Mr. Wonderful over to the rail and pulled him up. The colt's neck and flanks were lathered with sweat, and his sides were heaving.

"Oh, you poor guy!" Cindy sobbed. She had no idea how anyone could treat a horse like that, especially one as nice as Mr. Wonderful.

"You guys are always so sentimental about the horses," Brad said, swinging out of the saddle. "The idea isn't to make pets of them but to get them to run."

Mr. Wonderful dropped his head into Cindy's

hands. Cindy pressed her cheek against his soft forelock, trying to blink back her tears. When she looked up, she saw Len running toward them.

"What's going on with this horse?" Len asked sternly.

"He got some exercise for once." Brad was turning to go. "He has a long race ahead of him—he needs a hard work before it."

What race? Cindy wondered dismally, but she was too worried about Mr. Wonderful to think much about Brad's words. The Townsends were walking to their Ferrari without a backward glance.

Len shook his head. "Let's get this guy cooled out and rub some liniment on his legs. Don't look so worried, Cindy." Len patted her arm. "I think he came out of it all right."

"I hope so." Cindy forced herself to think about what they could do for Mr. Wonderful now, instead of her fears that he might be injured.

For the next hour she sponged the colt, walked him, and rubbed down his legs. Mr. Wonderful did seem to be okay, she noted with relief. He wasn't limping or even acting very tired. And the unfamiliar rider and harsh treatment just seemed to roll off him, unlike Glory. Mr. Wonderful was still his sweet self, bumping her affectionately with his nose as he followed her amiably around the stable yard.

An hour later Ashleigh and Mike looked into Mr.

Wonderful's stall. Cindy had just finished brushing the colt and put him up. She had done a thorough job, and the colt looked the way he always did. "Guess what—I just heard that Matchless won his allowance race at Belmont!" Ashleigh said cheerfully. "So how did things go here while we were gone?"

Cindy hated to spill the bad news. "Well . . . not so good. Brad stopped by and rode Mr. Wonderful."

Ashleigh's brow furrowed immediately. "Rode him? Where?"

"On the track." Cindy drew a deep breath. She might as well get it over with. She could hardly stand how disappointed Ashleigh was going to be that Cindy hadn't taken better care of the horses. "Brad breezed him."

Ashleigh stared at her in shock. "Without consulting me?" she asked.

"Let's take a look at the colt and see what the damage is," Mike said. His face was grim.

Cindy watched nervously as Mike and Ashleigh carefully examined Mr. Wonderful. As far as she could tell, he was perfectly fine. But she knew she might have missed something.

"He looks okay," Mike said. "Of course, we'll have to see how he comes out of it tomorrow."

"I'm so sorry, Ashleigh," Cindy said miserably. She hadn't seen Ashleigh so upset since Princess broke down in her race the previous spring. *No wonder,*

Cindy thought. *This is what happened to Princess all over again.*

"It's not your fault. I'm the one who should be sorry." Ashleigh seemed near tears. "I should never have given the Townsends a half interest in Glory. Look what's happened to Mr. Wonderful—nothing could be worse than this kind of treatment."

"I don't blame you," Cindy said quickly. She honestly thought Ashleigh had done the best she could with an impossible situation. Whitebrook couldn't lose Wonder's Champion to Townsend Acres.

Mr. Wonderful was standing quietly in his stall, looking from one of them to the next. He obviously didn't know what the commotion was all about, Cindy thought with a pang.

"Ashleigh, we've been over and over it—you had to do what you did with Glory," Mike said gently. "It's the Townsends who don't have to do what they're doing."

"I suppose." Ashleigh rubbed Mr. Wonderful's golden neck. She seemed to be trying to compose herself. "I just wish I could ride. Then the Townsends wouldn't have that as an excuse to exercise the horses themselves."

"You'll be back in no time," Mike comforted. "Just a couple more months."

"That's true. Our baby will be here in January." Ashleigh and Mike exchanged a smile.

As much as Ashleigh and Mike were looking forward to the baby, Cindy knew it must be frustrating to Ashleigh not to be riding. *Now might be a great time to give Ashleigh the present I bought for the baby*, Cindy thought. "Let's go up to the house," she suggested. "I want to show you something."

"Okay. I guess we've done all we can here." With one last look at Mr. Wonderful, Ashleigh slowly walked up to the house.

In her room Cindy looked under the sweaters in her drawer for the present. She'd bought it at the mall during the summer, and Samantha had told her to save it for a time when Ashleigh was feeling a little down. "I really think Ashleigh needs cheering up right now," Cindy murmured.

She hurried down the stairs with the brightly wrapped package. Ashleigh and Mike were sitting at the kitchen table, and the teakettle was beginning to simmer on the stove.

"Surprise!" Cindy said shyly, handing Ashleigh the package. "It's for the baby."

"Oh, Cindy, how sweet of you," Ashleigh said warmly. She tore off the paper while Mike poured hot water into three mugs. "Look, Mike!" Ashleigh held up the tiny tie-dyed sleeper. "Isn't this adorable?"

"It sure is," Mike said, joining them at the table. "Cindy, you didn't have to go to the trouble."

"But I wanted to." Ashleigh was still admiring the

sleeper. *I think I've gotten her mind off Mr. Wonderful,* Cindy thought.

But a moment later Ashleigh's expression darkened again. "I've really got to talk to Brad," she said. "Otherwise he'll just take Mr. Wonderful out again and do exactly the same thing. I'm afraid that at some point the tendon he injured is going to give out again. The next time, it may give out permanently and end his racing career."

Cindy cupped her hands around her mug. Despite its warmth, she felt chilled. If something wasn't done about Brad, Mr. Wonderful really might break down the way Princess had. Ashleigh certainly seemed to think so. Cindy shuddered as she remembered Princess's last race—the filly's leg almost shattered in two places, her searing pain, and her forced retirement.

Mike seemed to be remembering Princess, too. "Well, you can go over to Townsend Acres and see if you can get through to Brad," he said. "Or at least set some boundaries. We're co-owners of Mr. Wonderful— Brad can't arbitrarily exercise the colt any way he wants. I can't go with you right now, though. I have a meeting in ten minutes with several owners about next year's stallion seasons."

"I'll go with you, Ashleigh," Cindy volunteered. She had no desire to see Brad again, but she had to hear what was decided about Mr. Wonderful. *If Mike and Ashleigh can make Brad back down about Mr. Wonderful, maybe he'll leave Glory alone, too,* she thought hopefully.

Ashleigh was silent as she drove to Townsend Acres. But from her expression Cindy could see that Ashleigh was getting angrier by the moment.

At Townsend Acres, Ashleigh parked in the drive, hopped out of her car, and strode toward the nearest of the two training barns. Cindy hurried after her. That day she barely noticed the spacious, white-fenced grounds, stretching back almost as far as she could see and filled with top-quality Thoroughbreds, and the Townsends' imposing colonial house perched on the rise. Cindy had long ago stopped being in awe of the huge farm. Whitebrook might be a much smaller operation, but that year, with Glory and Shining both doing so well, Whitebrook was just as much the focus of the Thoroughbred industry's attention as Townsend Acres.

As Cindy stepped inside the barn she heard raised voices. Brad and Ashleigh stood in the aisle, arguing.

"I've held back for a long time," Ashleigh said angrily. "But you are not going to ruin Mr. Wonderful or Glory, either."

Brad had a small, superior smile on his lips. "So what's the problem here?" he asked with exaggerated patience. "I guess I just don't understand something. The colt's fine, isn't he? I don't know why you're getting so worked up."

Ashleigh swallowed hard. "It seems that way now," she said. "But if this continues—"

Brad held up a hand. "Mr. Wonderful went well today. I want to run him in a stakes race at Churchill Downs in November. Then he'll be in good shape for a campaign in Florida at Gulfstream. I've been in this business a long time, Ashleigh, and I know what I'm doing."

"We'll discuss that later. I want to talk about Glory, too," Ashleigh said doggedly. "We agreed that you wouldn't interfere with him, but you had him ponied in his last race. That might seem like a small point, but it upset him."

Brad seemed genuinely surprised. "I didn't arrange that."

"Oh, come on, Brad," Ashleigh said. "If you didn't, who did?"

Brad shrugged. "You can think whatever you want. You always seem to let your emotions get the best of you. But I've got work to do." He stepped into his office.

"Let's go, Cindy." Ashleigh turned on her heel. "I can't believe he would just lie to my face like that."

Cindy wasn't sure what to think. She had been around a lot of liars when she was in foster homes and felt she was a pretty good judge of when someone was lying. Unless Brad was the best at it she had ever seen, he *hadn't* been lying when he said he didn't arrange for the escort rider.

So what's going on? Cindy asked herself as she and Ashleigh walked back to the car. *Whatever it is, it can't be good for Glory. And it's not good for Ashleigh, either.*

8

"CINDY, DO YOU THINK HEATHER WOULD LIKE TO GO TO THE Breeders' Cup with us?" Beth asked as she ladled homemade vegetable soup into bowls for dinner the next Friday night.

Cindy stopped putting napkins on the table and stared at Beth in happy surprise. "Are you kidding? That would be so fantastic!" Then her smile changed to a worried frown. "But I don't think Heather can afford to come," she said.

"Don't worry about that," Ian said. "We worked out the cost for Heather's trip with her parents. It won't really cost that much to take her along—just plane fare and a few meals."

"Luckily, the airlines are having a fare war, so tickets are cheap," Beth added.

"Does Heather know?" Cindy asked excitedly.

"I think her parents are telling her now," Ian said with a smile. "They were going to talk to her when Mr. Gilbert got home from work."

The phone rang. "If that's Heather, don't stay on the line too long," Beth said. "We're about to eat."

"Okay!" Cindy dashed to the hall and grabbed the phone. "Hello?"

"Cindy . . ." Heather sounded so excited, she seemed hardly able to talk. "My parents say I can go to the Breeders' Cup with you!" she finished breathlessly.

"I know, Beth just told me. This is so great! You're going to love it at the track."

"What will we see first?" Heather asked.

"The horses," Cindy said quickly. "Glory and Shining and Matchless. Then we'll check out the whole field for the Classic."

"Do you know yet if Shining's running?" Heather asked.

Cindy felt some of her high spirits diminish. "Not yet. But when Sammy gets back from class tonight, I'm going to ask her. The Classic's a week from tomorrow, so she has to decide really soon."

"Tell me more about the track," Heather said.

"The most famous jockeys will be there, of course. Everyone wants to ride a horse in the Breeders' Cup. And there'll be a huge crowd."

"I'll bring my sketchbook," Heather said. "When Glory wins, I'm going to draw him crossing the finish."

Cindy suddenly had a vivid picture of Glory doing just that. She could almost see the flash of the jockeys' bright silks and hear the muffled roar of the horses' hooves as they plunged toward the finish.

"Cindy, are you awake?" Heather teased.

"Yeah, but I can hardly believe it." Cindy laughed.

After dinner Cindy went up to her room to do her homework. She tackled her history assignment first, since it was the longest and required her full concentration. After about half an hour Cindy could feel her head nodding. She tried to push on, though. The next day she and Heather planned to go to Mandy's jumping show, and Cindy didn't want to leave all her homework for Sunday.

Samantha looked in the door. "Hey, Cindy, how's it going?"

"Fine." Cindy quickly sat up straight at the sound of her sister's voice. Samantha looked cheerful and relaxed. The question of who was running in the Classic didn't seem to be bothering her.

"You're doing homework on a Friday night? Such dedication," Samantha teased.

"If I get my homework out of the way, I'll have all tomorrow to spend at Mandy's jumping show and with our horses." Cindy closed her history book. "I especially want to have enough time for Storm."

"He's doing so well for you." Samantha smiled

warmly. "You should just keep going the way you have with him." She sat on Cindy's bed, setting her books beside her. "I've got to finish up with things here, too," she added. "I'm heading up to Belmont tomorrow."

"Lucky you." Cindy looked at Samantha's thick textbooks. She thought that going to college must be a lot harder than being in seventh grade.

"I want to be at the track for Shining's last work before the race," Samantha said. "We'll probably time her on Wednesday."

"I think Shining and Glory are going to do so well in the Breeders' Cup," Cindy said hesitantly. "I can just picture Glory running so fast for the finish . . . and, well, Shining, too. . . ."

Samantha nodded. "Both of them are at their peak."

Cindy couldn't stand the suspense anymore, and Samantha didn't seem about to put Cindy out of her misery. "Which race is Shining entered in?" she asked.

"I haven't decided," Samantha said.

Cindy felt her shoulders slump. "But the Breeders' Cup races are a week from tomorrow!"

"I'll decide very soon." Samantha frowned. "Cindy, a lot of factors are going into my decision. It's not really the winning that's important in those races. I mean, it is, but—"

"Sure, I know." Cindy didn't want Samantha to go on. She knew her sister was right.

Samantha got up. "We'll get through this. After all, we're sisters. Sleep well," she said.

"You too." Cindy smiled gratefully at Samantha, then looked back at her history book. But she doubted that even history would put her to sleep now.

Cindy cupped her chin in her hands, trying to figure out how she felt about the Classic. *Glory's such a superhorse,* she thought. *I want more than anything for him to set records and win the Classic. It's so fantastic when he wins races. So why don't I feel good about it now?*

The next morning Cindy looked impatiently out the window of Beth's car at Heather's house. She could hardly wait to get to Mandy's show, but Heather wasn't ready.

"I wish Heather would hurry," she said to Beth. Beth had offered to drive Cindy and Heather to the show, which was being held about fifty miles away, near Louisville. Beth hadn't needed much convincing to take the girls. Since Beth had joined the McLean family, she had become an avid horsewoman. When her work permitted, she was nearly always willing to go to a horse race or show.

"Maybe Heather forgot something," Beth said. "Besides, we're late, too, Cindy."

"I know." Cindy sat back in her seat. She hadn't wanted to miss Storm's training that morning, and the

97

show had already started. Cindy hoped they would be in time for Mandy's class.

One of Heather's two little brothers, Ethan, ran over to the car. With his light blond hair and blue eyes, he was a small duplicate of Heather. "Heather'll be out in a minute," he said. "She's looking for her camera."

"Here I am!" Heather called breathlessly, slamming the front door and running down the steps.

"Mandy's parents will have a camera, you know," Cindy said as Beth headed the car for the highway.

"Yeah, but I want to take really special pictures of Mandy," Heather said firmly. "Hey, did you start that history assignment yet?"

"I almost finished it—then I started to fall asleep," Cindy said with a laugh.

"Well, explain it to me as far as you got," Heather said. "It looks hard."

During the car ride Cindy explained as well as she could their complicated assignment. It seemed that in no time they were pulling up at the show grounds. Hundreds of vans were parked in the grassy field surrounding the fenced outdoor ring.

"This is a big show!" Cindy said as she got out of the car.

"Yeah, and the riders aren't slouches," Heather agreed. "Mandy's really getting into serious competition."

As they walked across the show grounds, Cindy

thought how wonderful it was to be out in the chilly, invigorating fall day. The reds, golds, and browns of the changing leaves were bright and cheerful against the gray sky.

Near the stands a long table had been set up with lunch and drinks. The spicy scent of hot cinnamon punch wafted to Cindy's nose.

"Let's get some punch," she suggested.

"I'd love some," Beth said, shivering. "Brr! Feel that wind."

Cindy wrapped her hands around her cup of punch to warm them. Heather was studying a program. "Let's find Mandy and wish her good luck," Cindy said.

"Okay." Heather nodded. "She's probably in the practice ring warming up Butterball, since her class goes off after the one in the ring now."

"I'll get us seats in the stands and meet you up there," Beth said.

Directly ahead of Cindy a competitor was trotting her horse out of the ring after completion of her jumping round. Cindy admired the pair's sleek hunter look. The young woman riding wore a well-fitting black coat, tan breeches, and high, gleaming black boots. Her horse, a big bay, had its mane and tail braided with bright red ribbon. The classic formal English attire wasn't as eye-catching as the jockeys' flamboyant colors, Cindy thought, but there was a beauty and elegance to the English show scene, from the carefully dressed, neat riders to the tall, muscular horses.

The next competitors in the class were walking their mounts near the gate to keep them limber and to let off excess high spirits, Cindy guessed.

"What kind of horses are these?" Cindy asked Heather.

"Some are Thoroughbreds. Tor said a lot of them are warmbloods, too," Heather replied.

In the warm-up ring several ponies were already circling in preparation for the next class. Three practice jumps had been set up: a simple vertical, a two-foot-wide oxer, and a low combination.

"Do you see Mandy?" Heather asked.

"No, but she must be out here—she wouldn't miss a minute of practice time." Cindy scanned the ponies in the ring. All the riders looked older than her friend. "There she is!" Cindy pointed.

Mandy had just jumped Butterball over the combination. She cantered over to them. "Hi, you guys," she said.

Young as she was, Mandy always looked perfectly poised and in control on a horse, Cindy thought. "We just wanted to wish you good luck." Cindy patted Butterball's furry neck.

"Thanks," Mandy said. "I ride fourth—that'll help. I can see how the first three riders do." Cindy knew that after watching the other riders, Mandy would be able to spot problems with the course.

"Did you already walk the course?" Heather asked.

"Yup." Mandy looked nervous. "I should take Butter over one more practice fence before the class starts," she said.

"Okay. We'll see you in a bit." Cindy looked at Heather. "Let's go up to the stands and sit with Beth."

"We can sit on either side of her and try to keep her warm," Heather agreed. "It was nice of her to bring us here."

Beth looked distinctly blue when Cindy and Heather joined her in the stands. "I'll get you some more punch," Cindy offered.

"Thanks, Cindy—that would feel great." Beth smiled. "I really must be cold-blooded."

On her way to the punch table Cindy looked over at the ring, where workers had just finished setting up the course for Mandy's class. The attractive course consisted of eight jumps—two verticals painted in yellow and green stripes; three oxers, one of which looked to Cindy to be at least three feet across; an imitation brick wall bordered by boxes of flowers; a brush jump with a rail on top; and a gate, painted with flowers, that was swinging gently in the wind. Most of the jumps were about three feet high, Cindy guessed.

She paid for another cup of punch and hurried back to the stands, where she could see better.

"I feel warmer already," Beth said when Cindy handed her the steaming beverage. "Have a seat, Cindy. The class is just starting."

The first competitor rode into the ring. After circling his mount at a trot, he headed for the first fence.

His large liver chestnut pony lifted easily over the vertical. The pony seemed quiet and well schooled, Cindy thought. He and most of the other riders looked like tough competitors for Mandy.

"That rider looks about our age," Cindy said to Heather.

"I'll bet Mandy's the youngest in the class," Heather agreed.

Cindy watched tensely as the rider and his pony smoothly took jump after jump. She knew that if this rider went clean and Mandy did, too, they'd be in a jump-off. But Cindy wasn't sure if Mandy could compete against this boy. The three-foot fences would be so big for a pony Butterball's size.

"That rider's going off course!" Heather said in surprise, studying the diagram in front of her. "He missed a jump!"

"How could he make a mistake like that?" Cindy asked in astonishment.

"It's easy. There's so much pressure, and it's a pretty complicated course," Heather said.

At least with racetracks you can't get confused about the course, Cindy thought.

102

A bell rang, and the boy posted quickly out of the ring. He looked flustered.

"He's disqualified," Heather remarked.

"Poor guy," Cindy sympathized.

The next rider, a girl of about ten who looked a little big on her Shetland, knocked down the first jump and lost her composure. She and her mount went through the next two jumps and were disqualified. But the third rider, a blond girl on a Welsh pony, had a clean round. She rode out of the ring to loud applause.

"Here comes Mandy," Heather said.

Mandy entered the ring at a walk, then put Butterball into a trot. All her earlier nervousness seemed to have vanished, Cindy noted.

Mandy pointed the pony at the first vertical. Short as he was, Butterball made jumping seem effortless. With an easy rhythm Mandy guided him over jump after jump. A murmur of appreciation rose from the crowd.

Mandy flawlessly rode Butterball through a switchback and headed for the last jump, the colorful gate. Building speed, the pony narrowed the gap to the jump.

A gust of wind blew the gate backward, and it almost hit Butterball's knees. With a snort Butterball slid to a stop.

"He's refusing!" Cindy groaned. But the game little pony hadn't given up yet. At Mandy's urging and with a supreme effort he popped the jump, taking off from a standstill.

"They won't be penalized for that," Heather said excitedly.

"But Butterball refused the jump, didn't he?" Beth asked.

Heather shook her head. "Not unless he backed up. He can stop and take it like that."

Mandy finished the rest of the course and rode out of the ring to a burst of applause. She was grinning broadly.

Only two other jumpers in the class of ten had clean rounds. "Mandy's tied for first!" Cindy said.

"Now they'll go to a jump-off." Heather squeezed her hands excitedly.

"That was great!" Cindy grinned. She wasn't cold at all. She didn't think she could ever be cold while she was watching an excellent jumping exhibition.

Workers entered the ring and began rearranging and raising the jumps.

"They'll take out a few jumps and raise the rest for the jump-off," Heather said.

"What if more than one rider goes clean?" Beth asked.

"Then the rider with the fastest time wins," Heather said. "So the riders are going to be really flying if they can."

"As if they're racing." Cindy wondered if Mandy

and Butterball would be able to handle the tougher course. Butterball's hooves had come very close to some of the jumps in the first round. "Let's stand right next to the fence," Cindy suggested. "We can see better, and it'll be almost like jumping with her."

"Great idea! I want to take my special picture."

"I think I'll just sit here and use all these other people as a wind block." Beth laughed. "See you in a while."

Cindy and Heather threaded their way to the ring between competitors leading horses and the large crowd of spectators. A lot of people had apparently decided that watching a horse show would be a fun way to spend the gorgeous fall day.

"There's Mandy!" Heather pointed.

"Let's go wish her the best in the jump-off."

The younger girl's eyes were bright with excitement and tension. "That was kind of close with the gate in that last round," she said.

"You handled it perfectly!" Cindy praised.

"Good going," Heather agreed.

"Thanks, you guys." Mandy gave them a warm smile. "I'd better keep Butter moving," she added, gathering her reins. The small pony was prancing in place, sharing his rider's excitement.

"Let's go stand by the gate," Heather said. "It's the last fence in the jump-off."

"Okay." Cindy saw that workers had just raised

the top rail of the gate several inches. A total of six jumps had been raised or changed for the jump-off. Now the course consisted of a higher vertical, two broader oxers, the original combination with both elements raised, another raised vertical, and the gate.

Cindy looked into the ring through the boards of the fence and frowned. "That gate looks awfully high for a pony as small as Butterball," she said. "Mandy's going to have to take it exactly right to get over."

"I bet she will, though," Heather said.

Mandy rode first in the jump-off. She saluted the judges and put Butterball into a collected canter. The pony bounded over the vertical and oxers.

"What a great round!" Heather said admiringly. "She's such a natural!"

Cindy nodded. She could tell from her experience with racehorses that Mandy was riding very fast, right on the edge of losing control. *But maybe she has to or she won't win*, Cindy thought.

Butterball lifted over the first element of the combination. Cindy saw something bright fly through the air just as Heather snapped a picture. "He just lost a shoe!" Cindy said in horror.

"Mandy has to keep going." Heather's eyes were glued to the course. "She'll be disqualified if she stops."

As if nothing had happened, Butterball lifted over the last element in the combination and cantered on.

He took the final vertical, and Mandy pointed him at the colorful gate.

It's going to be okay, Cindy thought with relief. *Maybe it's not as serious to lose a shoe in a jumping competition as it is in a race.*

Butterball approached the gate. Cindy noticed that shoe or no shoe, Mandy hadn't slowed Butterball's speed at all.

But the pony stumbled on the takeoff. Before Cindy could even cry out, Butterball crashed through the gate, splintering it. Pieces flew everywhere, and the pony fell to his knees. Cindy saw to her amazement that Mandy did *not* fall. She urged the pony to his feet.

Slowly, with dignity and not looking back, Mandy rode out of the ring. "They've been disqualified," Heather whispered. "Oh, no!"

"We'd better go see how she's doing." Cindy was more worried about Butterball. He'd fallen hard on his knees.

Outside the ring Mrs. Jarvis was supporting Mandy by the elbow, and Mr. Jarvis was leading Butterball. The pony's head drooped, as if he was as disappointed in their performance as his young rider.

"Are you okay, Mandy?" Cindy asked anxiously.

Mandy shook her head. "I wrecked the beautiful gate," she said brokenly. "And we lost!" Mandy was so upset, Cindy couldn't tell which bothered her more.

"I think physically she and Butterball are all right,"

Mrs. Jarvis said softly. "But she's got a bad case of wounded pride."

"I do not!" Mandy cried.

"Should we come back in a little while, Mandy, when you're feeling better?" Cindy asked.

"No . . . I'm sorry I'm yelling about everything," Mandy apologized. "I just feel so bad. I thought the course was easy." The younger girl was brushing tears of disappointment from her eyes.

"Mandy, you had a really good round." Cindy tried to think what to say to make her friend feel better. "It was an accident that Butterball lost a shoe."

"I know." Mandy sighed. "I just get so mad when I lose. Not at Butter—he did his best. I want to try again."

"Of course you will," Mrs. Jarvis said. "But not today."

"At least this guy isn't hurt," Cindy said, running her hand down one of Butterball's legs. "We'll help you rub his legs down with liniment."

"Thanks," Mandy said in a small voice. "Poor Butter. I'm sorry, boy." She hugged the pony's furry neck tightly.

The small pony pushed his nose affectionately against her arm, as if to say that all was forgiven. Mandy took the reins from her father and with a determined nod set off for the Jarvises' trailer.

Mandy's so driven about jumping, Cindy thought as

she and Heather followed the Jarvises. *I guess that's what it takes to be a star. But I wonder if she tries too hard sometimes.*

Mandy's head was still down, and she was dragging her feet. "Poor Mandy," Heather said softly. "She looks so miserable."

Mandy's lost sight of almost everything but winning, Cindy realized. *And when she doesn't win, she doesn't have anything left.*

9

EARLY ON MONDAY MORNING CINDY WALKED STORM TO the track for his first exercise with other horses. The morning was cold and still, with a light frost dusting the tips of the grass and the dirt surface of the path. Cindy inhaled deeply, enjoying the icy sting of the cold air in her lungs. She could hardly wait to see how Storm would do in company.

"Are you ready for this, big guy?" she asked, leaning forward to run her fingers through Storm's silvery mane.

The powerful colt tossed his head and pranced a few steps, as if to say, *I never felt better.*

Cindy took up her reins on the off chance that Storm was feeling so good that he would try to bolt. But the colt already seemed to know the limits. He settled down into a brisk walk, craning his neck to watch

Landslide and Fortune's Paradise. Both two-year-olds, one chestnut and one bay, were already coming off the track.

Cindy dropped her heavy jacket on a nearby fence rail, moving slowly so that the flying piece of clothing didn't scare the colt. She had already been riding Storm for an hour, and despite the chilly temperatures she was thoroughly warm.

Cindy had gotten up two hours earlier, at three thirty, to exercise Storm by himself before he went out with the other yearlings. The sky had still been pitch black and hung with clear stars as she put Storm through a walk, trot, and canter in both directions. Then she had walked and trotted him in figure eights, working on his response to the reins so that he could be guided by just a touch. Storm had performed his lessons obediently. Cindy had done them all with him before, and the colt seemed to love to please.

"We'll try something new today," Cindy said. "I hope you do well exercising with the other yearlings, Storm, because this is real racehorse stuff." Most of what she had taught him so far could have been training for a pleasure horse. Cindy knew that from now on, Storm's behavior would be closely watched. Exercising in company on the track was a big step toward becoming an actual racehorse.

Ashleigh walked over to them from the mares' barn. Cindy pulled up Storm to wait for her.

"Is he doing okay?" Ashleigh asked.

"Really well." Cindy looked down to talk to her. Despite Ashleigh's obvious pregnancy, Cindy still couldn't get used to the idea that Ashleigh wasn't up on a horse anymore.

"Stay alert on Storm," Ashleigh warned. "A lot will be going on out here this morning."

Cindy nodded. "I'll watch him." She knew that Ashleigh was giving her extra words of caution because Cindy was very young to be riding a yearling colt. Ashleigh and everyone else sometimes worried that Cindy and Storm's inexperience might make a lethal combination.

I do have less experience than the other riders, Cindy thought. *I have to be careful not to go to sleep out here.* But she knew Storm so well, she doubted he had any unpleasant surprises in store for her.

Cindy stopped the colt at the gap to the track. In the predawn light the dirt was a muted purple, and the sky was a dark, misty blue-gray.

"Morning!" Vic called. Vic and Mark Collier, Whitebrook's other full-time groom and exercise rider, were leading the two other yearlings that would be exercised that morning—Secret Silence, a bay filly Mike had bought at the July select yearling sale at Keeneland, and Crimean Summer, a trade with neighboring farm Oakridge Meadows for one of Pride's stallion seasons.

Storm cocked an ear at the other yearlings but remained standing calmly. "Morning, Vic; morning, Mark." Cindy smiled with excitement. Riding with two such seasoned exercise riders, she felt like a professional.

Mike was already at the rail, waiting for them. Cindy had noticed that he never missed one of Storm's exercise sessions. She remembered that Mike had a special interest in sprinters. He had trained and raced Blues King, an excellent sprinter who was now retired to stud at Whitebrook. Mike thought they could make a sprinter out of Storm, too. Cindy knew that besides being an expert on training sprinters, Mike loved the explosive power of the extremely fast horses.

"Let's try just a walk, trot, and slow gallop today with the yearlings," Ashleigh said, leaning on the rail next to Mike. "Keep your distance from each other until we see how it goes. Take them out at a walk. At the quarter pole trot them three quarters, then gallop them slowly for a half."

"Remember to keep hold of them," Mike added. "We're not out here to race, but I have a feeling a couple of these yearlings are going to try to. We don't want them to go out of control and have to be yanked down. Even worse, they could go through a fence or into another horse and hurt themselves."

Cindy clucked to Storm, and the gray colt stepped off onto the loose dirt of the track. Cindy wondered how Storm would compare to the two other yearlings. She knew she wouldn't find out for sure that day, since she and the other riders would take the horses no faster than an easy gallop. Even when they breezed the yearlings, it would be hard for a long time to tell which had the most potential. Cindy knew that some horses matured faster than others, and they might have talent at different distances and over different surfaces.

Secret Silence was the most talked about yearling at Whitebrook. With four champions in her immediate pedigree, she was expected to make a splash on the track. And she did look like a champion, Cindy thought. The bay filly was beautifully compact and well proportioned. It didn't hurt, either, that she had a bright golden bay coat and a luxuriant black mane and tail. Secret Silence walked confidently onto the track.

"You'll do just as well as she does," Cindy said to Storm. Somehow she was sure of it. She loved riding Storm, especially with Glory away. She realized she had become very close to the darker gray colt.

Storm moved into the lead, walking faster than Secret Silence or Crimean Summer. Cindy cautiously guided Storm to the outside, keeping him well away from the other two yearlings. No one, not even Vic or Mark, knew what Secret Silence or Crimean Summer might do. Neither of them had been bred or raised at

Whitebrook, and they had begun their training elsewhere. Storm had been at Whitebrook only two months himself.

It's so special when the horses are homebreds, like Wonder's Champion, Cindy thought. *We know him so well. We'll be able to follow every minute of his training and races.*

At the quarter pole she asked Storm for a trot, according to Ashleigh's instructions. The colt surged forward, straining to get his head.

The sun was rising, spilling early pink light on the brown dirt of the track. Cindy squinted, checking to see that she was maintaining a good distance from the other yearlings.

Secret Silence was galloping up on Storm's inside. She wasn't supposed to gallop yet, Cindy thought with alarm. Secret Silence must have taken advantage of Mark's temporary blindness in the flooding sunlight and taken off on her own.

Storm jerked his head, pulling the reins through Cindy's hands as he tried to maintain his lead over the other yearling. Instinctively she tightened up on the reins and gripped hard with her legs to keep her balance. *Now what?* she thought, worried. *I don't want to discourage Storm from racing against other horses!*

"Pull Silence down into a trot, Mark!" Ashleigh called. "Don't let her take advantage of you!"

Cindy could see that Mark was trying to get a hold

on the headstrong bay filly. Finally Secret Silence dropped back into a nervous, quick-stepping trot, but she was slanting sideways across the track. Vic wasn't having an easy time of it with Crimean Summer, either. The high-spirited, nervous black colt was popping little bucks. Vic was expertly riding out the bucks and cueing the colt forward.

Cindy was proud that Storm was doing just what he was told, without trying any tricks. He never had—he'd been a dream horse to train. Storm had a nice disposition, but Cindy was sure that he had confidence in her because she'd spent so much time training him. He knew what was expected, and he wanted to please her.

They had reached the point where Ashleigh had asked them to gallop. *Now we can really go!* Cindy couldn't wait to see what Storm's action at the faster gait would be like on the track.

She looked left and right. The other two yearlings were right behind her, trotting at a brisk pace. They were a little close, Cindy thought, but they seemed under control. *Oh, well*, she reasoned, *they'll be galloping in a few strides anyway. Mark and Vic will straighten them out then.*

At Cindy's signal Storm burst into a gallop. "Slow down, boy—this isn't Derby day!" Cindy said, but she was enjoying the colt's eagerness. Shifting her weight in the saddle and adjusting her grip on the reins,

Cindy had plenty to do to keep the colt from galloping headlong down the track.

She heard thundering hooves behind them and looked quickly around. The two other colts had grabbed the bit and were roaring down the track, completely out of control! To Cindy's horror, both yearlings rushed in at them, Secret Silence from the inside and Crimean Summer from the outside. *I should have taken Storm away from them—now we're trapped!* she thought. *They're going to run into us!*

Cindy could see that both Mark and Vic were trying desperately to get the yearlings under control, but with the light bits used for training the colts, it was difficult. Secret Silence's shoulder bumped Storm's hindquarters, and the gray colt staggered. Struggling to stay upright in the saddle, Cindy wondered wildly what Storm would do. He might go crazy with fear. And Crimean Summer was right up there, too, grazing his other flank.

Storm seemed to be thinking about retaliating. He eyed the other horses, and his ears swept back.

"No, boy!" Cindy called, leaning over the colt's neck. "We're not out here to fight!"

Cindy let Storm out a notch to try to ease the traffic jam. She knew her move was risky. Storm might try to run off, and then three yearlings would be running wild instead of two.

With a snort of pleasure Storm drew away from the

bay filly and black colt. He settled into a smooth gallop. Cindy glanced over her shoulder and saw that Secret Silence was moving well now, toward the inside. Vic had finally managed to stop Crimean Summer by facing him into the rail.

"We did it, Storm!" Cindy called happily to the colt. She relaxed in the saddle, enjoying the brisk slap of the still chilly morning air on her face and the powerful, steady rhythm of the big colt's strides beneath her. The sun, well up in the sky by this time, cast a clear yellow light over the track, shimmering off Storm's dark gray coat. It was a beautiful day—and Storm was such a beautiful colt, Cindy thought.

Storm lugged in toward the rail a little. He seemed to be testing whether he could get his head, and Cindy thought she could sense the well-behaved colt's impatience with the lessons. He wanted to do what he had been born and bred to do—race his fastest.

"Just wait, boy," Cindy told the colt as she straightened him out. "You've done so well, in a couple of days we'll be galloping faster. Then we'll see what you can really do."

"Did you try putting the stirrups on the ball of your foot when you ride?" Cindy asked Laura at noon that day in the cafeteria. Cindy put her lunch bag down next to Laura's tray. Heather and Melissa were just setting their trays on the table across from them.

"Yes, I did adjust my stirrups." Laura sounded excited. "You know what? I forgot to do that at first with Angel Wings, the horse I was exercising this morning. He had his head down and was yanking at the reins when I galloped him. Then I moved the stirrups on my feet, and I was really able to collect him. My balance must have been about a hundred times better."

"Hey, that's good." Cindy was pleased that she had been able to help solve Laura's riding problem. But she was a little surprised that she knew enough about horses to tell other people what to do. She had only been riding about a year herself.

"How's your training with Storm going?" Max asked, sitting down in between Cindy and Sharon.

Glowing, Cindy related her morning training session with Storm's Ransom. "He was the best-behaved horse out there. So I'm going to gallop him faster in a couple of days," she finished.

"Wow, Cindy. That's absolutely thrilling. What can top personally training a horse?" Sharon asked with a sigh.

"I've got some exciting news," Heather said. "I'm going to the Breeders' Cup with Cindy!"

"Neat, Heather." Max sounded almost as thrilled as she was. "Are you going to help Cindy groom the Whitebrook horses?"

"I'd like to." Heather looked at Cindy.

"Sure," Cindy said. "You can help me walk Glory to the saddling paddock, too, if you want."

"Are you kidding?" Heather laughed. "Walk with a horse that's running in the Classic? I'd love to. I feel like a star already."

"Some people have all the luck," Melissa said. "I'm going to the Breeders' Cup with my family, but just to watch. We don't have a horse running in any of the races this year."

"There's one other thing I have to do at Belmont besides help with the horses," Heather said firmly. "I'm going to draw Glory winning. I said a long time ago that I was going to do it, and this year I will."

"Are you so sure Glory will win? Shining's running in the Classic, too, isn't she?" Laura asked Cindy.

Cindy looked at her hands to avoid Laura's gaze. "I don't know," she said.

"But how can you not know?" Sharon exclaimed. "Both horses are from your stable, and the race is in just five days—"

The lunch bell rang, and Cindy jumped to her feet with all the other kids in the crowded lunchroom. She was glad it was time to get back to class. Now she wouldn't have to answer Sharon. Her face burning, Cindy hurried into the hall.

"Good luck at the Classic," Max called, catching up to her.

"Thanks!" Cindy smiled. "I think every time you've told me good luck, Glory's won his race."

"Then I'd better keep doing it. What are friends for?" Max flashed her a smile back. "Aren't they supposed to cheer each other's horses?"

"Yeah." Cindy felt her smile slipping. *I always thought that's what friends are for,* she thought as she sat down in history class. *But I'm not sure what's going to happen Saturday with Shining and Glory.* She knew that Samantha would have decided by now which Breeders' Cup race to enter Shining in—she couldn't put it off any longer. But she hadn't told Cindy her decision, and Samantha had left for the track two days earlier. *I really don't know whether I can cheer for Shining if she beats Glory,* Cindy said to herself with a heavy sigh.

That evening Cindy sought out Ashleigh in the training barn. Cindy realized she couldn't stand not knowing which race Shining was running in. She figured Ashleigh must know by now.

Ashleigh was walking briskly down the stable aisle with a full bucket of feed for Crimean Summer. Being pregnant didn't seem to have slowed Ashleigh down much, Cindy thought.

"Ashleigh?" Cindy called. "Can I ask you something?"

"Just a sec." Ashleigh emptied the feed into

Crimean's stall, gently pushing aside the colt's eager nose. "Yes, Cindy?" she said as she walked back toward the feed room.

Cindy twisted her hands nervously. *How can I ask this without sounding like a jerk?* she wondered. "Is Shining going to run in the Classic?" she finally said bluntly.

Ashleigh stopped pouring grain into buckets and looked up. Her brow furrowed. "So you still don't know? Why didn't Sammy tell you?"

"I guess . . ." Cindy's words trailed off lamely. "I don't know why she didn't tell me. But what did she say?"

Ashleigh hesitated. Then she shook her head. "You should talk to Sammy about it," Ashleigh said firmly, scooping oats into Secret Silence's bucket. She picked up the bucket and headed back down the aisle.

Cindy trailed behind her. "But Sammy's already left for the track," she said miserably.

"Call her," Ashleigh said over her shoulder.

I can't. Cindy sat down on a hay bale in front of Storm's stall. *What would I say to Sammy if I called her?* Cindy wondered. *"I hope you're not running Shining in the Classic because I want my horse to win?" That sounds so selfish. But I have been selfish,* Cindy realized.

She got up and looked in on Storm. The charcoal gray colt was eating with gusto, pulling the rich green hay out of his net and tossing wisps of it. Despite her worries Cindy had to smile at the colt's enjoyment. "Pretty good chow, huh?" she asked.

Storm rolled a dark eye in her direction and ripped out another large bite. "I guess it's time for my dinner, too," Cindy said. "And I bet it's as good as yours." Beth had said she was making veal parmigiana and salad, but Cindy didn't feel hungry.

I really should call Sammy. But it's so hard to talk about serious things over the phone, Cindy thought as she walked back up to the cottage. *Besides, it's probably too late now to straighten things out with her. I should have talked to her about this weeks ago.*

The night was clear, and the stars twinkled brightly in the cold air. Cindy dug her hands into her jacket pockets to warm them. "I've messed things up so much," she murmured. "What if I don't know until race day, the biggest day of Glory's life, who's running against him in the Classic?"

10

"I'M GLAD BUTTERBALL CAME OUT OF THAT FALL AT THE show okay," Cindy said as she and Heather walked into the indoor ring at the Nelsons' stable on Wednesday. They had come to watch Mandy's jumping lesson. Cindy knew she was taking precious time away from her Whitebrook chores, but she thought Mandy needed support. The younger girl still seemed upset about her fall at the show on Saturday.

"Butterball's fine, but I don't think Mandy is at all." Heather sounded worried. "When I talked to Tor about what time I should come for my lesson today, he said Mandy seems depressed."

"I talked to her yesterday, and I could tell that something's really wrong," Cindy added.

"Hi, you guys." Tor waved to them from the far side of the ring. "Do either of you know what's bothering Mandy?" he asked as he dragged a crossbar to the center of the ring. "I know it has something to do with her fall at the show, but until I find out what, I don't know how to set up a jumping course for her."

"What do you mean?" Cindy asked.

"Mandy won't jump anything over two feet—or at least she wouldn't at her lesson yesterday," Tor said. "She just said she doesn't feel like going higher."

"She had a really bad fall," Heather said. "She's lucky neither she nor Butterball was hurt. Maybe she's kind of in shock."

"I wish I'd been there with her." Tor sounded concerned. "If I hadn't had to ride one of my horses in another show last Saturday, I wouldn't have missed it."

"Mandy had that other bad fall right after she first started jumping," Cindy said. "She almost gave up riding."

Tor nodded. "You did a good job of talking her out of it then, Cindy. Mandy has to be realistic. Nobody likes to fall, but if she wants to reach a professional level of jumping, she's going to fall sometimes. It hurts, but it happens."

Cindy shook her head. "I don't think that's her problem. Mandy's not really afraid of anything."

"No, you're probably right," Tor agreed. "If Mandy were afraid, she wouldn't have come this far in leg braces."

Cindy nudged Heather. "Here she is." Mandy stood

in the wide doorway to the indoor ring. She waved and walked toward them.

Cindy frowned. Mandy looked the same as ever, in her crisp tan riding breeches and polished black boots. But her face was glum, and she was walking heavily and a little awkwardly in her braces.

"This is almost the first time I ever noticed that Mandy wears braces—I mean, since I got to know her well," Cindy whispered. "She seems really unhappy."

"Yeah, she does." Heather looked worried.

Butterball followed Mandy at an energetic walk, bursting into a little trot now and then. He seemed eager to get going, but Mandy looked listless.

Why is Mandy acting like that? Cindy wondered. When Mandy had fallen badly at Tor's that other time, she had wanted to give up jumping because she thought she wouldn't ever be good at it. But after all her recent successes, surely Mandy couldn't feel that bad about losing one show. Cindy had thought Mandy had put all that behind her.

"Hi, everybody." Mandy's voice sounded flat to Cindy.

"Hi." Cindy studied Mandy's face. She noticed that Mandy wasn't looking her in the eye.

Tor gestured around the arena. Cindy saw that he had positioned only the standards of five jumps, putting the crossbars to the side. "What should I set up out here?" he asked Mandy.

"I don't want to jump over two feet." Mandy fiddled with Butterball's reins.

"Why?" Tor asked gently. "Where will that get you? You're not going to progress if we just stay at the same old level you were jumping at last year."

"But that's all I want to do." Mandy crossed her arms stubbornly.

"Okay," Tor said with a sigh. "Or maybe we should just concentrate on flat work today. We did the two-footers on Monday. I can't see much point in repeating that today. Let's just leave the jumps down."

Mandy hesitated, looking out at the jumps. "They look so empty without the crossbars up," she said sadly.

They did look awfully bleak, Cindy thought, just posts with holes in the middle. Even Cindy wanted to put the jumps together and make the course whole. "What's the matter, Mandy?" Cindy asked.

Mandy shrugged, pushing her fingers into Butterball's soft coat.

"You can tell us," Tor pressed. "That's the only way you're going to get past this, Mandy."

For a second Cindy thought the younger girl wasn't going to answer. Then she looked out at the jumps again and seemed about to cry. "I didn't act right at the show," she burst out. "I shouldn't have kept jumping when Butter lost his shoe. I should have taken him right out of the ring, even though we would have been disqualified. I knew he might fall if he didn't have a shoe."

"That was a judgment call," Tor reminded her. "You said the ground was a little slick. Your horse was missing a shoe. Maybe you should have stopped, but you used your experience and intuition in deciding to go on."

"But now I *know* I didn't do the right thing. Butter could have gotten hurt." Mandy sounded frustrated.

"He didn't, though," Cindy said. Now she understood better what was worrying her friend. Cindy remembered how she had felt after Princess's tragic accident on the racetrack—she had been terrified that Glory would get hurt, too. "Butter's smart and tough, Mandy. That's why you two have done so well."

"Butter wants to jump," Heather pointed out. The little pony was vigorously pawing the ground. Obviously he didn't understand why they needed to have a discussion about jumping.

"But I feel bad about something else." Mandy hung her head. "I was mean to you guys when you were trying to be nice after I fell." Mandy sighed. "That was awful of me."

"We understood how you felt," Cindy said. "Don't worry about it."

"You were just upset," Heather added. "We probably would have acted the same way if we lost after a great round like you had in the beginning."

"It was good until I messed up," Mandy said.

"Mandy, don't be so hard on yourself." Tor shook his head. "You made a mistake, but you learned from it. You're going to make a lot more mistakes if you go on in show jumping. As you gain experience, you'll make fewer mistakes and do better. And this time nothing's ruined beyond repair."

Mandy smiled a little. "Okay," she said. "I want to keep jumping. I love to jump so much. But I don't want to forget that I have to take good care of Butter."

"You won't," Cindy said quickly. "You'll never forget that."

"So, Mandy, how high should I make these jumps?" Tor asked with a smile.

Mandy seemed lost in thought for a minute. "Oh, about ten feet!" she finally said, flashing Tor a grin.

Cindy felt relief flood through her. *That sounds like the Mandy I know,* she thought.

"How about we start with two and half feet and go up to three?" Tor asked.

Mandy nodded briskly and lightly mounted up. As always, Cindy was amazed by how deftly Mandy swung her leg in the brace over the pony's back.

"I hope she does all right today," Heather said as Mandy rode off. "If she doesn't, she could lose her confidence again."

"She'll do fine." Cindy was positive that if Mandy

set her mind to something, there were no limits to what she could do.

Tor was setting up a six-jump course, a mix of a brush, a wall, and the usual crossbars and parallels. It wasn't a simple course of crossbars and parallels, Cindy noted. Tor wasn't babying Mandy just because she'd fallen.

"You can start, Mandy," Tor called.

Mandy hopped Butterball over the two low crossbars that Tor had set up as warm-ups. Then she pointed him at the first jump. It was an imitation brick wall, with the "bricks" painted in red on a white background. Visually the jump was daunting, but Mandy and Butterball took it with enthusiasm.

"Look, Tor just set up a gate." Cindy pointed. "It's about the same height as the one at the show."

"Oh, no!" Heather groaned. "I don't think Mandy should try to jump a gate today. I guess Tor doesn't know that's the jump she missed at the show."

"I'll bet he does." Tor was almost certainly trying to get Mandy past her fear so that she could move on, Cindy thought.

"I suppose Mandy won't have the same problem with that gate—I mean, the ground isn't slippery today." Heather sounded doubtful.

"And she's not competing," Cindy added. But she could feel her fists clenching with tension as Mandy rode up to the gate. It meant so much for her friend to succeed at this.

Butterball cantered straight at the jump. Mandy checked him a little with the reins, shortening his strides for a correct takeoff.

"She's pulling him up too much!" Heather whispered. "It's almost like she doesn't want Butterball to take it!"

"But she does want him to!" Cindy stared at the ring in frustration.

For a moment Butterball hesitated just a few strides from the jump. Cindy could almost feel the indecision in Mandy's hands. Then the game little pony gathered himself and lifted. He sprang over the jump, landed easily, and cantered on.

"Good boy, Butter!" Mandy's words of praise echoed in the large, high-ceilinged arena. "That was a super jump!"

"It really was," Cindy murmured. Mandy was so good, and she was so small, that sometimes Cindy could forget that Mandy was a little girl and Butterball was a pony. The girl-and-pony team reminded Cindy of riders in horse shows she had seen on television.

"Okay, rest him for a minute, Mandy, then take him around again!" Tor called. He walked over to Heather and Cindy. "What kind of spell did you put on her?" he asked with a laugh.

"No spell," Cindy said. "We just sort of sympathized."

"Well, Mandy listens better to you two about some things than she does to me." Tor looked thoughtful.

That's because I really do know how she feels—I should be saying all those things to myself about Glory, Cindy realized, feeling a knot grip her stomach. *All I've thought about is how wonderful it would be if Glory wins the Breeders' Cup Classic and goes down in history. But that isn't going to matter at all if he gets hurt. And what if Sammy never speaks to me again?* Cindy shivered.

"Look at Mandy go," Heather said admiringly. "She makes me want to get out there on my own horse and jump. It looks so fun."

Cindy nodded mutely. She had a feeling she hadn't made things very fun at Whitebrook. Mandy had apologized for not being nice to her friends at the show. Cindy still hadn't said anything to Samantha.

"When I get to the track, I'm going to talk to Samantha first thing," she said to Heather.

Heather nodded understandingly. "I think you should. You'll feel better."

"I'm going to tell her it's fine with me if she runs Shining in the Classic. I won't have any problem with it if Shining wins."

"I just hope you mean that," Heather said.

"Okay, Storm, this is a very big day—we're going to do your first long gallop in company." Cindy looked

132

between the colt's dark gray ears as she pointed him through the gap.

The weather had turned very cold the day before, and Storm arched his neck and snorted, his breath white in the bitterly cold early morning air. Cindy was sure from the colt's springy steps and the eager way he was looking around that he knew something important was up. "Let's make this training session a fantastic one, okay?" she said. "It's our last for a while. I've got to go back to Belmont tomorrow to be with Glory."

One of Storm's small, elegant ears swiveled as he listened to her familiar voice.

Cindy reminded herself not to expect too much that day. Storm was still very young, and one training session was never decisive in a racehorse's career—unless he had a terrible experience. Still, she hoped the colt would put on an impressive performance for his audience: Ashleigh and Mike, standing at the rail, and the two other yearlings, Secret Silence and Crimean Summer. Mark and Vic were already trotting the filly and colt on the track, keeping a good distance between them.

"Just a slow mile after a warm-up, Cindy," Ashleigh instructed. "And I mean slow. Don't let him get away—that could be disastrous. Start the mile at the quarter pole."

Cindy nodded and clucked to Storm, urging him through the gap. She knew from riding Storm these past months how much coiled energy the colt had. She would have to be alert every second to keep him under control. And even as nice a colt as Storm had his moods. Cindy would have to judge his reactions quickly.

She guided Storm to the outside of the track for his warm-up, where slower-moving horses traditionally went to avoid collisions. Storm's hooves crunched through a thin layer of ice. The sharp cold sliced through the blue stillness before the dawn, making Cindy gasp and numbing her fingertips as she put Storm through a thorough warm-up at a walk and a trot.

At the quarter pole she leaned close over Storm's neck, almost pressing her cheek into the colt's charcoal gray coat as she asked for speed. Storm bounded ahead, his strides smooth as he effortlessly reached for ground, as if he had been running on a track all his life. He was doing what he had been bred to do, Cindy realized. But he was doing it so perfectly!

Cindy heard the muffled pounding of hooves behind them. Glancing over her shoulder, she saw Mark moving up on Secret Silence. Cindy's heart thumped with fear. She wondered if the other yearling was thinking about bumping them or veering out of control, the way she had a few days ago.

"It's okay!" Ashleigh called. "Storm's got to learn how to move out a little in company. But watch his pace!"

Even if Silence does cause trouble, Storm and I have to

learn how to deal with it, Cindy realized. *But we're going so fast! We could really get hurt if we're bumped!*

Secret Silence was inching up alongside them on the outside, then she slowly passed them. "Are you okay, Cindy?" Mark yelled.

"Yes!" Cindy yelled back. The cold wind snatched the words out of her mouth.

A moment later she realized she had spoken too soon. Storm shivered. Either he was picking up on her nervousness or the sight of the other horse in front of them was too much for him to bear. In a split second he had grabbed the bit and roared down the track, leaving Secret Silence in his dust.

Don't panic, Cindy ordered herself. But she felt a shot of pure fear as the colt increased his pace still more. She was much more afraid for Storm than for herself. If he kept up this pace for long, he could hurt his young muscles, tendons, or bones for good. If he bowed a tendon, so that it would no longer support his leg properly, his racing career could be over before it started.

"Storm, stop!" Cindy cried, hauling back on the reins. "Don't do this!"

Miraculously the colt began to listen. His ears flicked back, and he dropped his pace a notch.

"Good boy!" Cindy said breathlessly. Her arms felt like rubber and her knees were a little weak, but it was all worth it. Storm was acting like a champion.

The colt settled into a rhythmic gallop, still pulling at the reins a little. The icy cold burned Cindy's nose and ears, but she felt nothing besides pure exhilaration. *Storm wants to run. So do I!* she thought.

But she knew that wasn't what they were out there for. Cindy guided Storm toward the rail, and he responded instantly to her touch. Suddenly Cindy felt utterly sure of herself on the colt. *I know this is what it's like to be a jockey*, she thought. *It has to be the best feeling in the world!*

She had felt like this with Glory—not only on the track, but also on the trails, Cindy realized. It was the same wonderful feeling of communion with her horse, of knowing exactly what he could do and what he was feeling.

Storm was still trying to get his head, craning his neck sideways a little and rolling his eyes to look at her.

"I know you want to run fast, but not today, boy," Cindy said. "You just have to be patient. I don't think I'll be breezing you until sometime in November. That's only a month away, though."

Shaking his head as if he disapproved of her restraint but was resigned to it, Storm completed the circuit around the oval at a controlled gallop.

"Very nice," Ashleigh said as Cindy rode over. "That was kind of a close call out there for a minute, but you kept him well in hand."

"That was good for him," Mike added. "The sooner

he gets used to moving quickly in company, the better."

"Sure," Cindy said, dismounting. She remembered Glory's troubled trip in the Gold Cup, when the other horses had run so close to him and bumped him. If Glory had been frightened by the contact, he would have lost the race. Now she had some idea of the terrifying crush of horses Felipe and Glory had faced out there.

Ashleigh was looking Storm over carefully. Cindy was sure that the young trainer wasn't missing an inch of Storm's well-muscled neck, shoulders, and hindquarters, rippling under his glossy gray coat. "Classy speed is prevalent in Storm's pedigree. But nothing in either his dam's family or his sire's indicates staying power," Ashleigh said thoughtfully. "We'll see how he goes. Even the speed isn't a sure thing—there's no telling yet. Buying an unraced horse is definitely a risk."

"So you don't think Storm's going to run well?" Cindy said uncertainly. She wondered if Ashleigh hadn't been pleased with the training session. "I think he's going to be really fast," she ventured.

Ashleigh smiled. "Oh, I do, too," she agreed.

That night Cindy opened her small suitcase to pack her clothes for the Breeders' Cup trip. She couldn't have been happier about the prospect of seeing Glory again.

Cindy took from her nightstand the exquisite silver bracelet from Ben Cavell, Glory's first trainer, and held it against her wrist. The bracelet was her good-luck charm. *To Glory, his and yours,* Ben had written when he gave her the bracelet. Cindy stared at the running silver horses encircling her wrist. They seemed never to stop.

"Cindy!" Beth called up the stairs. "Phone call for you."

Cindy shook her head, clearing it of daydreams. She hadn't even heard the phone ring. She picked up the hall extension.

"Hello?"

"Hi, it's me," Heather said. "What are you packing for the track?"

"Not much—we're only going to be there for three days. But take something nice to wear on race day. If one of the horses wins, we might be on TV in the winner's circle."

"Oh, right," Heather said seriously.

"But maybe it doesn't do much good to wear nice clothes around horses. I wore a great outfit for Glory's first race, and he shook mud all over it." Cindy laughed.

"I wouldn't care a bit. I can't believe I'm really going to the Breeders' Cup," Heather said.

"Me either, and I've known a lot longer than you that I'd be going. I've never been at the Breeders' Cup when a Whitebrook horse was running."

"*Two* Whitebrook horses," Heather reminded her.

"Yeah, two." Cindy was silent for a moment. She wondered again how she could solve her problem with Shining and Glory. Cindy supposed that she could find out which race Shining was entered in from the racing papers, but they might not have the latest information. Besides, she wanted to hear it from Samantha.

"Well, I'll see you tomorrow," Heather said.

"Bright and early," Cindy replied. "Mike, Ashleigh, Beth, and I will come by your house, and then we'll drive to the airport."

After Cindy had hung up, she looked at the picture on her nightstand of Ashleigh and Wonder in the winner's circle after Wonder's victory in the Classic. That year the race had been run at Churchill Downs. Staring at the familiar track, Cindy almost felt as if she could get inside the picture.

Maybe I can, she thought, opening a drawer in her bureau to take out a stack of sweatshirts. *I bet that's where I'll be standing with Glory on Saturday.*

11

"GLORY, GLORY BOY!" CINDY CRIED HAPPILY, RUNNING over to the colt the next morning at Belmont. Heather was close behind, carrying her sketchpad and a camera.

Cindy could hardly believe that she was really seeing Glory at last, after more than two weeks of separation. But there he was, right out in front of Whitebrook's shed row. Len was letting the magnificent colt graze on a small patch of grass. Glory sparkled a lustrous silver in the bright fall sunshine.

The colt's head shot up at the sound of her voice. He stared at her in amazement, as if to say, *I can hardly believe you're here, either!* A second later he pulled Len across the stable yard toward Cindy, whickering throatily.

"Easy, big boy," Len said with a laugh. "She's coming. There's no need to take me for a ride."

Cindy rushed to the colt. She didn't know which part of him she wanted to pat or hug first.

Glory seemed to understand. He rubbed his head against her shirt, then bumped her lightly with his shoulder. Cindy took his head in her arms and closed her eyes, lost in being with her horse. "There's so much to tell you," Cindy whispered, the words tumbling out. "Oh, Glory, I love you so much!" Sometimes Cindy thought that she could talk to Glory better than she could to any of her human friends. Glory was giving funny little whickers of joy, as if he had a lot to say, too.

"I think he missed you," Heather said with a laugh.

"You could conclude that," Len agreed.

"I know I missed him," Cindy said fervently. "How has he been doing, Len? Are the Townsends still working him too much?"

Len shook his head. "A bit harder than Ashleigh would like, I guess—but I don't think it's possible for a horse to look much better than this."

Cindy had to agree. From his soft gray nose to his thick, flowing tail, Glory couldn't look healthier or more fit. And now that she was around, he also looked like the happiest horse alive.

"Shining's going out for a breeze right now," Len added. "Do you want to watch?"

Cindy nodded. She thought she could tell from Len's kindly expression that he understood the situation with Glory and Shining without anything more being said.

"I'll hold Glory while you're gone." Len reached for the colt's lead rope.

"But I just got here—I can't leave him now." Cindy looked at her horse, torn.

"Go out and cheer for Shining," Len said firmly. "Glory will still be here in twenty minutes."

"I could take him with me." Cindy could hardly bear the thought of being separated from the colt for even a little while. They hadn't finished greeting each other at all.

"Leave him here," Len said. "The track officials don't want horses standing around and not doing anything. It just adds to the confusion, and there's plenty of that already."

"Okay." Cindy reluctantly handed Len the lead rope. She knew he was right, but she wasn't sure Glory would understand.

"There goes Shining." Heather pointed. Cindy turned and saw Samantha leading Shining to the track, adjusting a helmet over her auburn hair. Samantha was alone—Mike, Ashleigh, and Ian were probably already at the track.

"We'd better hurry or we'll miss the breeze." Cindy gave Glory a last pat. "I'll be right back, boy. I promise. I'm not going home this time or anywhere far."

The two girls hurried up the path toward the track.

Cindy couldn't resist looking back. Glory was staring after her, his expression half indignant, half quizzical.

"Be good," Cindy called.

Glory whinnied loudly, as if he thought her manners were terrible. Cindy stopped in her tracks, but Len waved her on.

"I guess he can live without me for another twenty minutes," Cindy said.

"Even if he doesn't think so," Heather agreed.

At the track Ian, Mike, and Ashleigh were closely watching the breeze of a smallish, powerful-looking black colt. They didn't notice Cindy and Heather's approach.

Cindy positioned herself along the rail so that she could watch, too. She could see that the horse was throwing everything he had into the breeze. It was Flightful, Cindy realized, Glory's main rival in the Classic—if Shining didn't run. No wonder everyone from Whitebrook was studying the black colt's performance.

"That's Flightful!" Cindy said to Heather.

"Wow!" Heather stared at the black colt. "He's pretty fast, isn't he?"

"Yeah, he is." As Cindy watched Flightful dig in with each stride, powering faster with every beat toward the wire, she understood why the black horse had awed racing crowds on the West Coast. "Glory's going to have to run a good race to win against him," she said. Her heart began to pound just thinking about it. In twenty-four hours it would be race day.

"He will," Heather said confidently. "And Glory's always beaten Flightful before."

"That's true," Cindy agreed.

Flightful shot across the finish line, and Ian half turned from the rail. "Hi, everybody!" Cindy called.

"Cindy! You're back." Ian smiled warmly and gathered her in his arms for a long hug. "You're just in time, sweetie—here goes Shining."

Ashleigh and Mike waved hello and turned back to the track. Cindy knew that small talk and catching up could wait until the important business of Shining's exercise was completed.

Blocking the sun with her hand, Cindy looked out across the track, too. Shining was a gleaming reddish streak trotting on the far side of the track among the many other horses exercising that morning.

"How's Shining doing?" she asked Ashleigh.

"She's fine." Ashleigh was looking through her binoculars.

"You don't usually breeze her this close to a race, do you?" Cindy asked. In at least some of Shining's races, she had come out of them badly tired.

"No, I don't. This will just be a short, quick breeze. I don't want to use her up, but it will get her on her toes for tomorrow," Ashleigh said.

Tomorrow. Cindy looked at Ashleigh, a question in

her eyes. What was the plan tomorrow for Shining? But Ashleigh was still gazing out at the track through her binoculars, and Cindy didn't want to interrupt her. Besides, Ashleigh would probably just tell her to ask Samantha.

"Here comes Shining!" Heather said. The roan filly was rounding the far turn, picking up the pace with each stride.

"She's flying!" Cindy gripped the rail with excitement.

Shining hurtled into the stretch, her head held high, her black and white mane whipping in the wind. Flightful's strides had been sure and determined, but Shining was all lightness and grace. Cindy couldn't believe how long the filly stayed in the air with each stride. She felt all her old love for Shining fill her, and tears came to her eyes. The sheer beauty of Shining's run was so amazing, Cindy couldn't want anything but for her to win whatever she tried.

"Shining!" she cried as the filly plunged toward the finish. "Oh, girl, you're incredible!"

Samantha lifted one hand briefly, and Cindy realized that she'd heard her.

Cindy dropped her head onto the rail. *If Glory and Shining run against each other and Glory's run is more beautiful, he'll win,* she thought. *If not, Shining will. But winning isn't the most important thing.* For the first time Cindy's stomach didn't churn at the thought of Glory losing. *I'm okay with whatever race Shining runs in now,* she thought.

Samantha rode through the gap. Shining was blowing lightly and skittering sideways a little with excitement from her run. Cindy went quickly to her head and held the reins while Samantha dismounted. "Thanks, Cindy," Samantha said.

"You're welcome," Cindy said shyly.

Shining's dark eyes were bright, and she was tossing her head. Obviously she had enjoyed her exercise.

Samantha looked at her horse critically for a moment, then turned to Cindy. "We need to talk," she said.

Cindy nodded. "I know."

"Let me get Shining cooled out, then let's go to the beach," Samantha suggested.

"Great—I've never been there!" *But maybe this isn't going to be fun,* Cindy thought. *Sammy may be mad at me.* She realized that the way she had been acting had spoiled not just going to the beach but a lot of things—how she felt about Glory's and Shining's races and her relationship with Samantha.

"It's way too cold to swim, or I'd suggest you go with us," Samantha said to Heather.

"I understand," Heather said quickly. "I don't mind hanging out here at all."

"Let's go tell Glory where we're going," Cindy said.

"Then I bet Len would like some help with the horses while Sammy and I are away, Heather."

"I'd love to help him." Heather nodded. "And if he doesn't need help, I'll draw."

"I'll meet you two back at the shed row," Samantha said.

As she and Heather walked back from the track, Cindy wondered what Samantha would say. *Maybe I should be the one to talk first*, she thought. *I've got some explaining to do. And apologizing.*

Len had put Glory back in his stall while they were at the track. At the sound of Cindy's footsteps the big colt popped his elegant gray head over the stall door.

"Hi, gorgeous," Cindy said, stepping closer to rub his forehead. Heather walked down the stable aisle, patting the eager noses of Matchless and Whitebrook's other two allowance horses.

Cindy spent the next half hour with Glory in his stall, getting reacquainted. First she brushed his coat to relax him. He didn't need to be brushed to clean him—the colt didn't have a speck of dirt on him. Then she vigorously stroked Glory's burnished coat with a finishing cloth until his dappled coat glistened like polished silver. She finished off the grooming with a big hug.

Glory leaned gently into her arms, rubbing his ear gently against her shoulder. Glory couldn't talk, but Cindy knew that he was telling her how much he loved being with her. Heather sat on a hay bale, sketching Matchless's head.

"Are you ready, Cindy?" Samantha asked, looking over Glory's stall door.

Glory jerked his head and stepped to the door of the stall, standing alert. Cindy wondered if she'd been wrong and Glory *could* understand words. "I know—I'm going away again and you don't like it," she said.

"I'll be here, Glory," Heather offered.

Glory eyed her, as if he were dubious about whether she would do as a substitute. Then he accepted a piece of carrot and a caress from Heather. But as Cindy left the barn the colt gave a piercing whinny that tugged at Cindy's heartstrings. As often as she had to leave him, she still wished she could always be with him. And Glory had no idea where she was going. He didn't know that she'd be back soon—or if she'd ever be back.

"I thought talking would help us sleep tonight, if anything can before a big day like the Breeders' Cup," Samantha said with a laugh as they walked to the car. She stopped in the parking lot and looked directly at Cindy. "Let's get this all cleared up, shall we?"

"Yes," Cindy said. She realized that she had been dreading this moment for months. But now that she and Samantha were really going to talk, she felt wonderful.

12

CINDY WALKED BESIDE SAMANTHA ON THE WET SAND, enjoying the deserted, windy beach. The cold, blue-gray water of the Atlantic Ocean crashed in high waves along the shoreline, and seagulls called raucously overhead. A flock of sandpipers chased the receding waves, and Cindy ran along the water's edge with them, daring the waves to wet her feet. She lost the bet a couple of times.

"It must be so much fun to swim here when the weather's warm," Cindy said to Samantha.

Samantha was carrying her shoes and nudging mounds of crushed seashells with her toes. "Yeah, I'll bet it is," she said absently.

Cindy looked sideways at her older sister. *Sammy's never even been a little mad at me*, she thought. *What if she's really mad now?* Suddenly Cindy lost her appetite for playing in the ocean. She remembered Samantha's unfailing support since the night Cindy had arrived at Whitebrook, a runaway orphan looking for a bed. Without Samantha's help, Glory wouldn't even be at Whitebrook—Samantha was the one who had ridden him and shown Mike and Ian what the colt could do. She had always been on Cindy's side—until now.

Cindy felt tears burn her eyes. *I just found a sister a year ago,* she said miserably to herself. *Have I lost her already?*

"Let's sit for a while," Samantha suggested.

Cindy sat beside her in the dry sand beyond the waterline and picked up a handful of sand. She wondered if it was too late to tell Samantha that she knew she'd been a brat. But Samantha didn't look angry, just thoughtful. Gathering her courage, Cindy opened her mouth to tell Samantha that it was fine by her to run Shining in the Classic.

"Let me think how to put this," Samantha said.

Cindy leaned back against a low dune and waited, letting the sand run through her fingers. She noticed that on the horizon a lone sailboat with a striped sail was struggling against the wind.

Samantha looked out to sea, too. "Cindy, I'm not running Shining in the Classic," she said.

"You're not?" Cindy looked at Samantha in astonishment. She could hardly believe her ears. Since Samantha hadn't said anything about the Breeders'

Cup races for so long, Cindy had just assumed Samantha was trying to spare her the bad news that Shining and Glory would be rivals.

"It makes much more sense to enter her in the Distaff," Samantha explained. "If Glory and Shining both run in the Classic, the best finish we can hope for is one-two. Whitebrook would just lose the chance for two first-place finishes in the Breeders' Cup races."

"But . . . why did you say, right after she won the Whitney, that you were thinking about entering Shining in the Classic?" Cindy asked.

Samantha frowned. "I guess at that point I wasn't sure Glory would be running in the Classic. Things weren't going so well for him—he'd just lost the Jim Dandy. That was what first put the idea into my head. That, and Shining's wonderful performances in the Suburban and Whitney against colts."

"Shining's the best racehorse ever," Cindy said earnestly. She had never meant anything more in her life. "I mean, except for Glory. . . ." Cindy trailed off, confused.

"The two aren't mutually exclusive." Samantha looked directly at Cindy. "Cindy, for me what's important is working with the horses and my relationship with them. Of course I like to win, but it's not essential."

"I think I understand that now." Cindy dropped her eyes. "I guess I didn't for a while, though."

151

"Look at it this way. You're so patient in training Storm," Samantha reminded her. "You haven't lost sight of what's important there—training him to be the best he can be and enjoying the love you two share. Even if Storm never wins at the track, won't what you've done with him be worthwhile?"

Cindy thought of the sleek, well-mannered, loving charcoal gray colt. "Of course," she said. She knew she wouldn't trade success at the track for a minute of that wonderful relationship.

"Well, it's the same thing with Glory—winning just isn't everything."

"I know, I know." Cindy sighed. "Oh, Sammy. I'm really sorry. I want Glory to win so much. But, well, I forgot that other things are important, too. More important than coming in first."

"Good," Samantha said. "Because you can't always win. Not even with Glory, not even with Shining."

Cindy dug her sneaker into the sand. "I'm still not sure if I understand one thing."

"What's that?" Samantha asked.

"Don't you want Shining to . . ." Cindy couldn't think for a moment how to say it. She cleared her throat. "Well, you know, win the Classic, and have everybody say she's the greatest racehorse in the world?"

"Cindy, Shining already *is* the greatest racehorse in the world—to me," Samantha said firmly. "Another

152

win more or less isn't going to change that. And I feel the Classic is Glory's race. Besides the Classic, there really isn't any other Breeders' Cup race to enter him in—the other races are on turf or are for younger horses, except for the Sprint. The Distaff will definitely showcase Shining's talents. It isn't an easier race than the Classic—it's a mile and an eighth, against the best fillies and mares in the world. But I'm confident Shining will hold her own."

"So am I! It'll be incredible if Glory wins the Classic and Shining wins the Distaff!" Cindy tossed a handful of sand into the air.

"Won't it?" Samantha smiled at her.

Cindy smiled back. Suddenly the colorful sailboat on the horizon, the surging, whitecapped surf, and the acres of smooth, deserted sand looked bright and cheerful to Cindy. *I'm never going to let anything come between me and Samantha again*, she thought. *No horse race is worth that—not even the Breeders' Cup Classic!*

The second Samantha pulled up in the Belmont parking lot, Cindy threw open the car door and hurried to the shed row. She could hardly wait to see Glory again. That wasn't unusual, especially given their long separation, but this time she had a new reason for wanting to be with the colt. She felt that she owed him an apology just like the one she'd given

Samantha. She hadn't appreciated him enough for what he really was.

"He might even be mad at me for running off and leaving him again," she muttered as she walked quickly between barns. "We barely got to say hello, and then I rushed off again."

In the shed row Cindy saw to her surprise that Ian and Len stood in front of Glory's stall. That wasn't so unusual, but she couldn't understand what they were doing. Glory was trying to lip Ian's shirt while Len firmly rubbed the colt's neck. As Cindy came closer she saw that Heather and Ashleigh were in Glory's stall, also patting the colt. Glory was fidgeting.

"What's going on?" Cindy asked. Glory blew out a sharp snort, as if to say, *Well might you ask.*

"He was pacing and fretting, so Heather went in the stall," Ashleigh said. "He didn't stop, so *I* decided to tend to him. That didn't help much, either."

"Once four of us were around, he settled down." Ian eased his shirt out of Glory's mouth. "Kind of settled down," he added wryly.

"I guess four people were enough attention," Heather said.

"Probably just one is enough, now that Cindy's here," Ashleigh pointed out.

"I'll take over," Cindy said, grinning.

"Good." Ian laughed. "You're the new baby-sitter. We've all got things to do."

"I'll stick around for a while," Ashleigh said. "I want to keep an eye on our champs, Glory and Shining."

"You need lots of eyes on you—you're trouble, aren't you?" Cindy said lovingly to her horse.

Glory tossed his head and checked the pockets of Ashleigh's jacket for carrots. He seemed completely unrepentant about disrupting everyone's schedule.

Cindy took a lead rope off the hook. "How about if we go outside and have a little grass?" she asked Glory.

"I'll bet he'd like that," Heather said.

Suddenly Glory pricked his ears.

"What is it?" Cindy looked around and saw Brad and Lavinia Townsend walking down the aisle.

"Not them again," Cindy muttered. She hoped they wouldn't upset Glory. He needed to stay calm and relaxed for the race the next day.

Heather made a sympathetic face. "Maybe they won't stay long," she whispered.

"That would be a first," Cindy whispered back. Glory leaned over the stall door and bobbed his head. He was so friendly, he seemed pleased to see his visitors, Cindy thought. Glory had never really had the problem with the Townsends that everyone else at Whitebrook did.

"We'd like to see the horse, please," Lavinia said to Cindy. Cindy noticed that Lavinia was wearing riding clothes instead of one of her usual designer outfits.

Maybe, Cindy thought, Lavinia had noticed that the dress was a little more casual in New York than at the Kentucky tracks. Lavinia had always looked absurd to Cindy, walking around the stable in her fashionable clothes.

Cindy glanced at Ashleigh to see what she should do. Ashleigh nodded imperceptibly, and so Cindy led Glory out of his stall.

The gray colt stamped his foot and looked eagerly around. Cindy knew that Glory associated going out of his stall with good things—exercise on the track, walks around the shed row, grazing, and, possibly his most favorite thing, warm sponge baths. He wasn't expecting to just stand there and be inspected by the Townsends, she thought.

"Glory's gained weight," Brad said. "It's all muscle, too."

Cindy noticed that Ashleigh had moved away, but she hadn't left the barn. Cindy thought she knew why. She didn't trust the Townsends, either.

"I'm not sure what the best racing strategy would be for Glory tomorrow," Brad said thoughtfully. He walked around the colt, examining him closely.

"Glory certainly did well in the Gold Cup when he took the lead early." Lavinia brushed a speck of dust off her breeches.

Glory stamped his foot again and yawned, showing all his teeth clear back to his throat. Cindy almost laughed. Sometimes Glory did that when he had food stuck in his mouth. But in this case it looked as though the Townsends weren't impressing him at all.

"Let's talk tomorrow," Brad said to Ashleigh.

"All right." Ashleigh nodded. Cindy was a little surprised that Ashleigh didn't say more than that.

With a big sigh of relief that the ordeal of the Townsends was over, Cindy gave Glory a carrot. She figured he deserved a treat just for giving them that great yawn.

"See you in the winner's circle," Lavinia said to Ashleigh as she and Brad walked out of the barn.

"We'll be there," Ashleigh replied lightly. Mike, who was just entering the barn, waved at the departing Townsends.

Heather laughed. "Is Lavinia trying to sound like a horseperson?"

"I guess." Cindy bit her lip nervously. She hoped Brad wouldn't wear himself out thinking of new ways for Glory to run the next day.

"Well, Brad's training ideas seem to have resulted in a very fit horse," Ashleigh said, as if she guessed what Cindy was thinking. "The times for Glory's works have really raised eyebrows around here. Of course, the true test of our strategy will be the race tomorrow."

"Are the Townsends going to mess up Glory's run?" Cindy asked worriedly.

"No, of course not," Ashleigh said reassuringly. "I just spoke to Clay Townsend, and he couldn't be happier about what we've done with Glory."

"And he's still the boss at Townsend Acres, whatever Brad pretends," Mike remarked.

"I wish Brad hadn't had an argument with Felipe a couple of days ago, though," Ashleigh said. "Around horses, Felipe's one of the gentlest and most tolerant jockeys I know, but he doesn't always have much patience with people. I guess Brad was giving Felipe unwanted advice about how to ride. Felipe told him that he takes orders only from us. Brad, of course, flew off the handle."

"I can understand Felipe's point," Mike said. "He doesn't want to be bombarded with instructions from all sides."

"Well, he and Brad almost got into a fight." Ashleigh frowned. "That wouldn't have been good in itself, but Felipe might also have been suspended. We certainly can't afford to have that happen now and have to find a replacement jockey for Glory. We know how Glory acts with strange jockeys."

"Oh, no!" Cindy burst out. Before they had found Felipe as Ashleigh's replacement, Glory had thrown, intimidated, and otherwise acted terribly for over a dozen jockeys. Felipe was their last hope.

"Don't worry, Cindy—it didn't happen," Ashleigh reassured her. "Felipe's still riding."

"Think about the race," Mike advised. "If Glory wins it, he'll be a definite contender for Horse of the Year."

"Really?" Cindy asked excitedly.

"Possibly." Ashleigh looked thoughtful. "Glory's had such an up-and-down career. I don't really know how the committee will view the race he won when he tested positive for drugs. I know they won't count it as a win, but I don't think it will count against the horse as a deliberate drugging, since our stable wasn't implicated."

"I think everything depends on Glory's Breeders' Cup run," Mike said. "If he puts in a performance to remember here, that will be foremost in the voting committee's minds when they select the Horse of the Year."

Cindy knew what Mike meant. If Glory set a record in the Classic, he would probably win Horse of the Year honors.

Glory was breathing softly, contentedly into Cindy's hand. Cindy made a decision. The next day was a very big one. She needed to give Glory whatever edge she could, and he was always more relaxed when she was around. She had to stay with him as much as possible from now until the race.

"Heather, do you want to spend the night here with Glory?" Cindy asked. "I think he needs me. But you don't have to stay if you don't want to. You could go back to our room at the motel."

"Of course I want to stay," Heather said quickly. "It'll be cool to spend the night with the horses. But what will we sleep on?"

"I can find you a couple of spare cots," Len said, approaching them with a bale of hay. "You're not worried about anything, are you?" he asked Cindy.

Cindy shook her head. She knew Len was referring to the last time she'd slept in Glory's stall—when he'd been drugged, and she'd needed to protect him. But maybe she still felt that way when Glory had a big challenge ahead, Cindy thought.

"Will your parents let us stay out here?" Heather asked.

"I think so." Cindy wasn't sure if she would get an argument from her parents or not. She hoped they were used to the idea.

When Cindy talked to Ian and Beth about an hour later, she was pleasantly surprised to find that they had anticipated her.

"We knew you girls would want to sleep here," Ian said. "So this time we came prepared—we brought you both sleeping bags and foam mattresses."

"You're going to look a little rumpled in the winner's circle," Beth said with a smile. "But who cares, right?"

Cindy smiled back. *So Beth is sure Glory will win, too*, she thought. Cindy was glad her parents were so understanding.

"Let's sleep in *front* of the stall," she said to Heather. "Otherwise Glory might try to play with us all night. The last time I spent the night here, he slept for only about an hour, at least that I saw. He needs his rest for the race tomorrow."

"Okay," Heather said. She giggled. "Or we could go in the stall next door and pretend to be horses!"

Cindy grinned. "I think I *am* part horse. But we'd better stay in front of the stall, not next to it, so Glory can see us."

After a quick dinner at the track kitchen Cindy and Heather spent the next few hours helping make sure the horses were comfortable for the night. With Len, Cindy checked that the bridles and saddles, leg wraps, and other equipment were clean and in good order for race day. Heather went down the row of stalls to see that all the horses had plenty of fresh, soft bedding and water.

"Okay, kids—we're going back to the motel," Beth said, looking through the barn door. "Len will be sleeping in the feed room, and there's a security guard out front if you need anything."

"We'll be fine." Cindy smiled. This was so different from the last time she'd slept in the barn at the track. Glory was safe, and he couldn't be in better shape for his race. Cindy felt a quick flicker of nervousness at the thought of the effect of Brad's training on the colt. But Ashleigh seemed satisfied with Glory's condition.

Things are going so well, Cindy said contentedly to herself. Best of all, she and Samantha were all right with each other again.

"What do you want to do?" Heather asked, snuggling into her sleeping bag. "Hey, this is pretty comfortable."

"We should sleep soon." Cindy yawned. "We've got to get up at four."

"Ooh. Makes me tired just to think about it."

"Yeah, but the morning's nice." Sometimes it was hard to leave her bed at first to take care of the horses, especially in the cold winter months, but within minutes Cindy was always glad she had. She liked hearing the first chirps of the birds and the eager whinnies of the horses as the day began. The next morning, the morning of Glory's biggest race day yet, would be the nicest so far, she thought.

13

Cindy woke very early. Out the barn door a sliver of pale orange light in the east, banked by gray clouds, was the only sign that morning had come.

She got up to check on Glory. The gray colt was sleeping peacefully in a corner of his stall with his head low and all four legs braced. Cindy smiled and tiptoed away.

What a wonderful dream I had, she thought as she carried her small suitcase to the bathroom to change and wash up. Cindy had dreamed that she was cheering Glory on in the Classic, telling him to run as if he had wings. Then she had seen that he *did* have wings—long, beautiful silvery ones. *Maybe it was only a dream, but I think the race today is going to be big,* she told herself.

Cindy decided to walk around the grounds for a

while until the horses' feeding time. She didn't want to wake up Glory or anyone else. Heather was still sound asleep deep inside her sleeping bag. Even Len wasn't up yet.

Lights were on in a few of the shed rows, but the backside was almost still as Cindy walked through the stable yard. Cindy stuck her hands in her pockets and shivered, half from cold and half from excitement. It was such an important day for Whitebrook, she thought. Very soon it would begin for Shining and Glory.

Cindy stopped in front of the black statue of Secretariat, the legendary winner of the Triple Crown. *It's so amazing that Glory is running at this track, where horses like that have been*, she realized. *He's one of them!* Cindy felt a burst of pride and delight.

"This is going to be the biggest race of your career, Glory," she said softly. "And I'll be so proud if you win. But you know what? That's not the most important thing to me at all. I just want you to come home safe and sound so that we can go on those winter trail rides I've been thinking about."

Cindy realized she should head back to the barn. Probably the others would be waking up by now—including Glory. She noticed that the early morning clouds had blown off, leaving a clear pale blue sky. It looked like a perfect race day.

Len was up and preparing the morning feed when

she reached the Whitebrook shed row. "Morning," she said.

"Morning. You're up early, aren't you?" Len smiled.

Cindy shrugged. "I couldn't sleep. But Glory sure could."

Len nodded understandingly. "Take this to the big guy," he said, handing Cindy a bucket with only a small amount of grain. "Not too much for either Glory or Shining this morning."

"Glory will know it's race day, since he's getting a small breakfast." Cindy took the bucket and started down the aisle.

Len chuckled. "Oh, he does already. One of the birds told him, I guess. He's raring to go."

The big gray colt had seen Cindy and was eagerly hanging over his stall door, looking for his breakfast. "Len, I really think he's going to win today—by a lot," she called over her shoulder. Then she wondered if she should have said that. After all, no one ever really knew what would happen in a horse race. *Maybe I just think Glory will win because I love him so much*, she thought.

"That boy's headed for Breeders' Cup glory," Len said firmly. "There's no doubt in my mind."

Heather was sitting up in her sleeping bag, yawning.

"Morning," Cindy said cheerfully.

"Are you sure it's morning? I think it's too early."

Heather yawned again. Then she rolled back her sleeping bag and hopped up. "Just let me get changed, then I'll help you feed the horses."

"Great." Cindy quickly poured Glory's breakfast in his stall before the colt got any more agitated.

"Hi, everybody," Samantha called as she came down the aisle with Ashleigh and Mike. "Let's start getting Shining ready for the Distaff right after she eats," she added.

Mike laughed. "You're not anxious, are you?"

"Nope," Samantha said firmly. "I just want to be prepared."

Cindy noticed that Samantha didn't seem the least bit nervous about the Distaff. That seemed strange to Cindy. Samantha had always been extremely nervous before all Shining's races, and this was the biggest race of Shining's career.

I wonder if Sammy gave herself the same talk she gave me, Cindy thought suddenly. *Maybe I wasn't the only one who cared too much about winning.*

Shining would run in the Distaff before Glory went in the Classic. The Classic was the last race on the card and would go off about five o'clock.

"I don't know if I can wait more than twelve hours for Glory to run in the Classic," Cindy said.

"Well, we've got a lot to do before then," Samantha said.

"That's true." As Shining's groom, Cindy would be

busy helping to get the roan filly ready for her race. And throughout the day Cindy wanted to help Glory to peak mentally. Physically the gray colt couldn't be more fit. But by walking him around the stable yard, talking to him, and just being with him most of the day, Cindy thought she could get the colt in a relaxed, confident mood to take on the Classic field.

"I cleaned Shining's saddle." Samantha stroked the soft leather of the tiny saddle. "I wanted to do a special job, so I took it back to the motel last night."

"Did you clean it so well because you're planning for Shining to be on TV?" Len joked.

"Maybe." Samantha smiled.

"I'm planning to be right there in the winner's circle with Shining," Ashleigh said. "Even though I'm not sure I'm looking my best these days."

"I'm sure you are," Mike said fondly, putting his arm around her.

Cindy looked in Shining's stall. The beautiful filly was cleaning the last bits of feed from her tray. Cindy was glad to see that Shining's appetite was good— she would definitely need her strength on the track. "Let's get you out and give you the brushing of your life, girl," she said.

Shining obligingly stepped to the stall door and nudged Cindy. *Today Shining seems as calm as Samantha,* Cindy thought. *That's good.* Sometimes before races Shining had been wired, wasting energy.

"Let's all groom her," Samantha said with a warm smile. "She'd like that."

"So would we," Heather said shyly.

"I really think Shining's chances are fantastic today." Samantha handed brushes to Cindy and Heather. "She beat colts at a mile and an eighth in the Whitney and at a mile and a quarter in the Suburban."

"I agree," Cindy said enthusiastically. Her heart was already pounding with excitement. *And the day is just going to get more wonderful from here,* she thought.

The morning passed quickly. With Heather's and Samantha's help, Cindy brushed Shining until the filly's coat was as soft as silk and every single red and white hair gleamed. Shining basked in the attention and soothing brushing. She half closed her eyes, leaning into the brush when Cindy hit a favorite spot.

"Let's go watch the Sprint," Cindy said to Heather after they had eaten the sandwiches Beth brought for lunch. Cindy jumped up, brushing off her jeans. They had been sitting in front of the shed row in the cool fall sunlight. "I think we're done around here for now."

"Sounds good to me." Heather nodded.

"Let me just ask Sammy if it's okay if we go." Cindy had her own special reason for wanting to watch the Sprint. With Storm's breeding, he would probably be a sprinter. She wanted to see the best sprinters in the world run.

Samantha had put Shining back in her stall and was

sitting on the straw, keeping her horse company. Ashleigh was looking at Shining over the stall door.

"By all means, go," Samantha said when she heard Cindy's plans.

"You should like the Sprint," Ashleigh added. "Those horses really burn up the track. Running a sprint is much different from running a longer race—speed is all."

"But do you need us here?" Cindy looked at Samantha questioningly.

"Not right now. I'll stay with Shining," Samantha said. "A little time with just me around would probably be good for her. Besides, I've seen a lot of Breeders' Cup Sprints. Not that I wouldn't like to see another one, but I should spend quality time with Shining."

"Okay." *That's what Glory needs, too,* Cindy said to herself. *I wonder if I should stay with him.* For a moment Cindy couldn't decide. But it was important for Storm that she watch the Sprint, she reminded herself.

Glory was watching her calmly from his stall. "He seems fine now that he sees you every day," Heather said.

"Yeah, I think so, too. I'll be back soon," Cindy promised the colt.

"We'll come get you if he seems upset," Ashleigh said reassuringly. "Go enjoy yourself. This is Breeders' Cup day!"

"Come on," Cindy said to Heather. "Let's stand

169

right at the wire." Cindy always sat in the stands when one of the Whitebrook horses was racing—it was too hard to see the whole race from ground level. But nothing was more thrilling to her than standing right at the finish, just yards from the winning horse in its moment of triumph.

"Yeah, let's stand close," Heather agreed. "I want to get a really good look at the horses."

Cindy noticed from the board that seven horses were entered in the Breeders' Cup Sprint. She and Heather positioned themselves at the finish line, slipping between taller people. "There go the horses for the post parade," Cindy said. "I can hardly see them, though."

"Too many people in the way," Heather agreed.

The crowd parted for an instant, and Cindy caught sight of a breathtaking gray. The superb filly was prancing and pulling on the reins, obviously anxious to run.

"I hope that gray wins," Cindy said. She didn't know who the filly was, but Cindy liked her attitude and color.

"Me too," Heather said. "She's so beautiful."

The horses loaded in the gate, but Cindy couldn't see much of it since the gate was on the far side of the track. The bell rang distantly. "There they go!" Cindy picked up her binoculars.

"And it's Missy's Chieftain off to an early lead," the

announcer called. "Sailing Free is a close second as they head into the turn!"

"That's the gray on the lead!" Heather said.

"Yeah! She's a powerhouse—look at those fractions!" Cindy said admiringly. "The pace is unbelievable!" She could never believe how fast the fractions were in sprints. Unless a horse like Just Victory was running, the fractions at classic distances were usually slower. "I can see why Mike likes sprinters," Cindy added.

"And they're coming into the stretch!" the announcer called.

"I can still hardly see them," Heather said.

"Listen!" Cindy had a big grin on her face. "They're coming, all right."

There was no mistaking that sound. Seven Thoroughbreds were pounding for the finish line, their hooves hitting the ground with a roar like a freight train.

The gray filly was still on the lead, blazing along the track. The horses plunged across the finish. "Missy's Chieftain won!" Heather said.

"I know!" Cindy hoped that it was the day for gray horses to win at the races. She smiled. It was hard not to be a little superstitious at the track. "We'd better get back to Shining," she said. "The Distaff goes off soon."

Samantha had Shining crosstied in the aisle, and she and Ashleigh were polishing Shining's hooves.

"Need help?" Cindy asked.

"No, thanks—I'm about done here." Samantha stood up. "The horses were just called to the saddling paddock for the Distaff."

"Okay!" she said with a bright smile. "Let's take Shining out."

As they led Shining to the saddling paddock people were packed around the walking ring, waving their programs and shouting. Cindy wondered what all the excitement was about.

"What's going on?" Heather asked. "I mean, everyone was pretty noisy before, but they just got incredibly louder."

The crowd's roar swelled, and Cindy could make out some of the words. "Everybody's cheering Shining!" she cried.

Samantha had tears in her eyes. "I can't believe it," she said.

"Well, you should," Ashleigh said. "Shining's got a huge fan club."

"It means so much to get this kind of reception for a Kentucky horse at a New York track," Samantha said.

"A lot of people here love horse racing," Mike said.

"And Shining!" Cindy grinned, running her hand over Shining's silken shoulder. Shining was high-stepping and arching her lovely neck. Cindy thought the roan filly was giving the crowd just what they'd come to see.

Ian and Kelly Morgan walked over to join them. The young jockey smiled nervously. "This is the biggest day of my life! I hope I can do justice to Shining."

"Of course you can," Ian reassured her. "Shining's been going very well with you aboard."

"Ride her just the way we talked about this morning, Kelly," Ashleigh said. "Shining likes to run on or close to the lead, so I'd risk letting her out a little too much rather than take the chance of getting trapped behind the other horses. Keep her to the rail if you can—I think the track's favoring inside speed today."

Kelly nodded. "All right."

Cindy thought that Kelly would do fine—she was an excellent rider. Cindy was glad that Kelly had kept riding for Whitebrook even after the problems she'd had with Glory.

Ian gave Kelly a quick leg up into the saddle. Shining sidestepped, the muscles in her shoulders and hindquarters bunching. Then she stood very still and craned her neck around to touch Kelly's boot. Shining blew out a little snort and turned toward the track. She seemed to be saying, *Now that I'm sure who's on my back, I'm ready to race.*

"Okay, girl," Kelly said with a firm nod. "Let's show them how to run!"

"Shining's on her way," Samantha said. "Let's get back up to the stands and check out the field."

In the stands Beth passed out drinks to everyone. "I saw Shining's reception in the walking ring on a TV monitor while I was getting the drinks," she said. "Sammy, honey, you must be so proud!"

"I was," Samantha admitted. "And a little dazed. I think I still am. Shining's going to run in the Distaff!"

"I got us drinks because I thought we'll all have sore throats soon," Beth said with a laugh. "We're going to be doing a lot of cheering!"

The ten horses in the Distaff walked onto the track. Cindy frowned. Just going by appearances, she thought every single one of the elegant, spirited horses out there could win the race. "How does the field look to you, Sammy?" she asked.

"Good and bad." Samantha was carefully studying the horses. "Grayson's Delight, that bay with two white socks, has a thin racing record. She's won only two races, and one of them was just an allowance race. But I'm not counting her out completely. She's a daughter of Grayson's Knight, a sire of top fillies. I noticed in the walking ring that she's very well balanced."

"Other contenders in this race are more formidable," Ian said. "Winning Reprise is coming off a definitive win in the Beldame at a mile and an eighth."

Cindy saw Winning Reprise, a light gray with a darker mane and tail, loading in the number-one position in the gate. *I guess I'd better hope that for this race, it isn't a gray-horse day,* she realized.

"Her time wasn't nearly as good as Shining's in the Whitney, which is the same distance as the Distaff," Samantha said.

"It didn't have to be," Ian remarked. "She was so far ahead in the stretch, her jockey pulled her up to save her."

"I guess I knew that." Samantha's forehead creased.

"I didn't mean to scare you, honey," Ian said comfortingly. "Kelly knows to watch out for Winning Reprise."

"Look at those odds!" Mike pointed to the board. "Shining's going in as the heavy favorite."

"That's wonderful." Beth smiled and reached across Ian to squeeze Samantha's shoulder.

Cindy smiled, too, but she knew the odds weren't nearly as good on Glory in his race. He would probably be going in as the favorite, but Flightful, Chance Remark, the winner of the Belmont, and Treasure's Prospect, the champion from Florida, were close behind.

One race at a time, she told herself. Cindy firmly put Glory's race out of her mind as the fillies and mares loaded in the gate for the Distaff. She wanted to cheer for Shining one hundred percent.

Cindy balanced her soda on her knee and stared intently at the track, where in just seconds Shining would be running. She could feel the soda jiggling slightly because her hands were shaking. It meant so much to her for Shining to do well in this race—for Samantha's sake, and for everyone else who had followed the roan filly's career and loved her.

At the bell Shining broke cleanly and surged to the front. "Go!" Cindy shouted in delight. "That's the way, girl!"

"She's got command of the race already!" Ashleigh cried.

"Now if she can just hang on to it . . ." Samantha gripped her soda so hard, it almost spilled over the sides.

Cindy could see that Shining had every intention of doing just that. With authority she increased her lead to three lengths. But as the horses headed into the turn Grayson's Delight was up pressing at Shining's flank. Kelly let Shining out a notch, and the roan filly drew off.

"Don't use her up," Samantha said tensely. "She's still got a long way to go!"

It looked to Cindy as if Shining was easily maintaining her lead, but she was only two lengths ahead. That was by no means a comfortable margin. Almost every horse in the field was still within striking position.

"Shining has ripped through the early fractions," the announcer called. "The rest of the field is forced to stay with her, but Grayson's Delight is faltering!"

The bay filly was dropping back, Cindy saw, and so were almost all the other horses. But Winning Reprise was making her move—she was starting to close! The gray filly slowly ate into Shining's lead until the two horses were neck and neck. Kelly was pressed flat against Shining's back, asking for every ounce of speed that Shining had.

"Come on, Shining girl," Cindy screeched. "Don't let her beat you!"

As if the roan filly had heard, she dug in, reaching for ground. Slowly Shining drew away to a length lead.

"She's going to do it!" Samantha cried.

"And that's not all!" Ian said.

At the three-eighths pole Shining seemed to decide to put the competition away for good. She lengthened her strides still more and charged for the finish.

"And Shining has seized control of this race!" the announcer's voice blared.

For a moment Cindy couldn't speak. Shining's effort was so generous and so beautiful, it hardly seemed to matter that she was flying toward the finish.

"Shining guns down the stretch to win by five lengths!" the announcer shouted.

"She led wire to wire!" Cindy cried. "Oh, Sammy, this is so wonderful!"

"Isn't it?" Samantha's eyes shone. "Let's get down to the winner's circle, everybody!"

Kelly rode Shining to the side of the track. She was

smiling broadly. "I've just ridden a Breeders' Cup winner," she said. "Thanks so much, Shining!"

Cindy quickly looked Shining over. The roan filly was breathing fast but lightly, and her coat was hardly marred by sweat. She had come out of the race so well, she almost seemed not to have run it.

Cindy gripped Shining's bridle firmly, trying to get her to hold still for the winning photo. Shining tugged at the reins and squirmed as a track official laid the winner's blanket of purple and yellow flowers over her withers. She looked ready to run another race right away, Cindy thought. "You'd better stop it," she said, her loving tone softening the words. "Do you want a blurry picture in every paper in the country?"

"Samantha, after a performance like Shining just gave us, any regrets you didn't run your horse in the Classic?" a reporter asked.

Cindy looked quickly at Samantha, worried that she would see some sign of remorse on her sister's face. But Samantha's expression was radiant.

"I didn't feel the Classic was Shining's race at this time," she said simply.

"Shining had a dream trip today. What kind of a race do you think March to Glory will run in the Classic?" one of the reporters asked. "Do you think he'll coast to victory?"

"We're confident he'll run a strong race," Ashleigh said.

"And what do you think?" the reporter asked Cindy. "As Glory's groom, how does he seem to you today?"

The reporter's black microphone was just an inch from Cindy's face, and she gulped. She knew that every word would be transmitted across the country. "I think Glory's ready," she said carefully. "I think he'll run like he has wings."

"So there you have it from Cindy McLean, one of the people who knows March to Glory best," the reporter said, turning from Cindy.

Cindy's cheeks flushed with excitement. *Wow, he really listened to what I said, just like I was a trainer!* she thought.

"Well done, Cindy," Ashleigh said affectionately. "You're already a pro with the press."

Samantha turned to her. "So, shall we start getting Glory ready for the Classic?" she asked.

Cindy nodded, already looking to the backside. Her throat was too tight to speak. She swallowed hard with excitement, anticipation, and nervousness. Would she be back in the winner's circle with Glory soon?

"Do you really think he'll coast to victory, the way those reporters said?" Cindy asked Ashleigh anxiously.

"I hope so." Ashleigh's forehead wrinkled. "Or he may have to run the race of his life."

14

"YOU KNOW YOUR BIGGEST RACE EVER IS COMING UP, DON'T you?" Cindy asked Glory.

The gray colt snorted, his hindquarters dancing in the crossties. Cindy could hardly reach him with the finishing cloth. "Okay, okay," she said with a laugh. "I guess you answered my question—you want to get out there." Glory was acting every inch the spirited Thoroughbred that he was, she thought with satisfaction.

"He wants to race," Heather agreed.

Ashleigh walked down the aisle with Len. "Time to go to the saddling paddock," she said, smiling at Cindy. "Are you nervous?"

"I'm a lot more nervous than Glory." Cindy gave the colt a final rub with the finishing cloth before he could jump away again. Then she clipped a lead line to his halter. She looked at Ashleigh. "What do you think the race will be like?" she asked.

"The Classic is always a challenging race, but the competition is even better than usual this year," Ashleigh said thoughtfully. "Fortheloveofit, the number-four horse, won the Hollywood Futurity at two and at three won the Santa Anita Derby, among other stakes. He's got a lot of early speed, but I think Glory can outlast him. Chance Remark won the Belmont this year and obviously can go the distance. Treasure's Prospect was champion older horse last year. And Flightful is always a tough contender. Glory's beaten him several times, and so ordinarily I wouldn't be that concerned about him, but—"

"But?" Cindy said. She felt her stomach flutter. She couldn't believe the credentials of Glory's competition.

"Darby Stables, one of the stables Joe Gallagher trains for, is running a double entry in the Classic— Flightful and a three-year-old colt named Wild Reason," Ashleigh continued. "Wild Reason hasn't raced much."

"But isn't that two against one?" Cindy asked.

"It could be." Ashleigh raised an eyebrow. "We'll have to see how the race plays out. Of course, if Glory has a rough trip, it could be anybody's race."

Cindy frowned. That didn't sound good.

"Don't worry, Cindy," Ashleigh said reassuringly. "I don't think Glory's in over his head."

"I don't, either." Cindy looked at Glory. He had a distinguished racing record, too, she reminded herself. "Ready?" she asked him, unclipping the crossties.

Glory lifted lightly on his hind legs and stepped eagerly toward the barn door.

"He's ready," Len confirmed with a laugh.

The walking ring was mobbed with people standing several rows deep. It was even more of a madhouse than it had been earlier in the afternoon, Cindy thought.

"People are almost crushing each other trying to see Glory!" Ashleigh said over the cheers, greetings, and general roar of conversation.

"Yeah, it's pretty amazing!" Cindy was holding Glory tightly, and Len had attached an extra lead line to Glory's halter and was walking next to him on the other side. Cindy knew that nobody wanted to take a chance that Glory would get loose and rush into the crowd. Heather followed Cindy, carrying her sketchbook and pencil case.

In the saddling paddock Len quickly adjusted the saddle on the colt's back. Then Len guided him to the walking ring, where Ian, Mike, Ashleigh, and Felipe were waiting. Cindy felt a surge of pride when she saw that Felipe wore the blue-and-white silks of Whitebrook. She knew that one of Ashleigh's stipulations in selling the half interest in Glory to the

Townsends had been that the colt race under Whitebrook's colors.

Felipe mounted up swiftly and patted Glory's neck. "You got any last words for this guy?" he asked Cindy. The jockey's expression was serious, and Cindy felt pleased. *Felipe really wants my opinion!* she thought.

Cindy hugged Glory's head. "I think you know what to do," she said. With his usual sweetness, Glory stopped his racehorse prancing and fidgeting and tucked his head deeper into her arms. "Run for it!" she whispered. "Make it Glory day!"

"You listen to her, big horse," Felipe said, affectionately patting Glory's shoulder. "See you soon at the wire," he added to the Whitebrook group. Cindy thought both horse and jockey looked confident as they rode toward the tunnel to the track.

Ashleigh smiled. "I was just remembering my ride in the Classic on Wonder," she said. "I was scared and green, but Wonder brought me through."

Cindy watched Glory's flowing tail swish as he walked to the track. She felt a lump form in her throat at the colt's cheerful, energetic attitude. She was sure that Glory would try his best that day, just as Wonder had. *And that's enough, no matter what happens,* she thought, turning to follow Ashleigh to the stands.

"Glory's the most beautiful horse here," Heather said.

"I think so, too." Cindy tore her eyes away from

Glory and smiled at her friend. "Let's find our seats."

Samantha and Beth were already up in the grandstand. "Look, Glory isn't being ponied today," Cindy said as she sat next to Samantha.

"Thank goodness." Beth looked around Samantha to talk to Cindy. "He definitely didn't like it the last time."

"Don't anyone faint, but I just found out I actually wronged Brad about that," Ashleigh said. "It was Lavinia, not Brad, who arranged for Glory to be ponied in the Gold Cup. Of course, Lavinia wasn't going to tell us that."

Cindy frowned. *Why would Lavinia have Glory ponied when everyone knows he does better without an escort?* she wondered. *Lavinia couldn't want to sabotage Glory's chances now that he's a Townsend Acres horse, too.* Then Cindy remembered how inexperienced Lavinia was around horses. "Do you think Lavinia thought she was helping?" Cindy said tentatively.

"Maybe." Ashleigh sighed. "It's possible that I've been wrong about a lot of things the Townsends have done."

"What do you mean?" Mike sounded surprised. Cindy noticed that Glory was gliding to the starting gate, the picture of ease, good breeding, and grace. He seemed to be saying, *I have this race in the bag.*

Ashleigh hesitated. "I was talking about what

184

happened to Princess," she said. "Psychologically, that was such a horror for me. Brad's probably right that I never got over it the way I should have. I was too quick to blame, and I've been tentative in my training of other horses since Princess got hurt."

"But Princess's injury *was* Lavinia's fault," Samantha pointed out. "She rode her so badly."

"Yes, but Brad said Lavinia honestly believed there wasn't much to exercise-riding a horse as nice as Princess is. Lavinia didn't understand that Princess is probably the most wired of any of Wonder's offspring, certainly much more than Wonder herself. Then—" Ashleigh shrugged. "Lavinia didn't want to admit how wrong she'd been."

Cindy was silent for a second, thinking about Princess's shocking tragedy. She couldn't blame Ashleigh for being slow to forgive. Heather looked at Cindy with her eyebrows raised, as if she too wondered if Ashleigh could really do it.

"I suppose Lavinia's entitled to one mistake—I just wish it didn't have to be Princess," Ashleigh said sadly.

Mike squeezed her hand sympathetically. Ashleigh shook her head and smiled. "But we've got other things to think about now, don't we, like our baby and Glory's race. The horses are going to the post for the Classic!"

"Glory's *trotting* into the gate," Cindy said in delight. "He can't wait to run!"

"He's got quite a race ahead of him," Ian said tersely.

The fourteen horses in the field seemed to Cindy to take forever to load into the starting gate. Wild Reason and Flightful, the double entry from Darby Stables, were the 2a and 2b horses. Fortheloveofit was in the four hole, and Glory was in the five hole. Chance Remark and Treasure's Prospect were the eleven and twelve horses.

"Much as I'd like the race to get under way, the delay in starting might actually be to Glory's advantage," Ashleigh said.

"Glory's never had a problem with standing in the gate," Cindy agreed. Cindy knew that most horses began to fidget and lost their concentration if they had to stay in the gate for long.

The gate slammed on the last horse. A bare instant later the bell clanged and the horses rushed out of the gate, a closely bunched blur of brown, black, and gray.

"Glory's in second!" Cindy shook her head in dazed disbelief. "How did Fortheloveofit get ahead of him? Glory broke well from the gate!"

"It's early in the race yet," Ashleigh reminded her. But Cindy could see that Ashleigh's mouth was tense as she scanned the field.

"And it's Fortheloveofit off to an early lead. Back half a length is March to Glory," the announcer called. "But here comes Wild Reason, already making his move!"

186

In the next second Wild Reason powered into the lead and drew off. Fortheloveofit was half a length back in second, and Glory was third by several lengths. Chance Remark and Treasure's Prospect were trapped behind other horses, but that was no comfort to Cindy. "Fortheloveofit and Wild Reason are beating Glory!" she cried in agony. "No, this can't be happening!"

"And the two speedballs, Fortheloveofit and Wild Reason, have set blistering early fractions!" the announcer called.

"Look at the time for the first half!" Mike said grimly, gesturing at the board.

"I was afraid of that." Ian groaned.

"What's the matter?" Cindy asked frantically.

"The long-shot horse, Wild Reason, was entered to set very fast early fractions," Ian said. "He'll fade, but he'll take Glory with him, or any horse that tries to keep up. Then a closer—his stablemate, Flightful—will take command of the race."

"Isn't that illegal?" Cindy asked in horror. Glory was pressing close at Fortheloveofit's flank. He would never let the other horses stay in front. He'd burn himself out!

"No, it's not illegal," Mike said tensely. "The fast horse is called a rabbit."

Cindy could hardly stand to watch. Felipe had succeeded in rating Glory just off Fortheloveofit, but Cindy could see that Glory was upset at being checked. He was throwing up his head and getting rank as he fought for rein.

Hauling against Felipe's hands, Glory closed furiously on Fortheloveofit and put the chestnut colt away. Then he set off after Wild Reason.

"Felipe just let Glory out all the way—he took off like a shot!" Samantha said.

"He had to. Glory wouldn't stand for any more restraint." Ashleigh hadn't taken her eyes off the track.

Glory swept by the bay colt on the outside, but he didn't slow, Cindy saw. Her heart was in her throat. *What are you doing, Glory?* she thought desperately. *You're out in front. Slow down!*

"And it's March to Glory blazing into the lead by two lengths!" the announcer called.

"That was a suicidal third quarter!" Samantha gasped. "Glory can't possibly keep going that fast! Felipe has to slow him down."

"He can't!" Ian said. His face was as worried as Samantha's.

Cindy watched Glory closely for signs of strain. Glory was so fast, Cindy was sure that it wasn't the times on the board but how her colt was running that mattered. Glory was almost floating, his long legs effortlessly eating up the ground. The rest of the pack was far behind, except for Flightful—the black colt was running on the inside about four lengths back. The rabbit, Wild Reason, had faded to sixth.

Slowly Cindy's hopes began to rise. "Glory's okay!" she shouted jubilantly. The board flashed a roaring eleven and three-fifths seconds for the last eighth of a mile, but she could see how easily and beautifully Glory was running. Out of the corner of her eye Cindy saw that Heather had her sketchpad out and was drawing quickly.

"Here comes Flightful!" Samantha cried.

The black colt had begun to close. Cindy held her breath. This was the moment when Glory would either fade or keep up his blinding speed. But she knew in her heart what the gray colt would do.

"He's determined to stay in front!" Mike shouted. "I just hope he doesn't kill himself!"

Cindy took a sharp breath at his words. *But I know Glory can do it*, she thought.

"Glory can stay long distances," Ashleigh said. "He's going to blow the race open!"

Flightful was chasing Glory with everything he had, but Glory continued to draw away. As Cindy watched the two horses round the far turn, screaming herself hoarse along with the rest of the crowd, Flightful dropped back a length. Glory didn't slow. In fact, Cindy could see from the board that he was running even faster.

He's running for himself now! Cindy thought, her heart thumping with joy. Flightful was falling farther and farther back as Glory pounded into the stretch.

"March to Glory is picking it up as he heads for home!" the announcer shouted. "He's the runaway leader—he's got twenty lengths on Flightful now!"

Cindy squeezed her hands until her knuckles hurt. Glory was going faster with every stride. *I'll never see anything so wonderful again,* she thought.

"Glory is going for a world record—under a hand ride!" the announcer cried.

Cindy saw Felipe start at the announcer's words and look at the board, checking the fractions. Then he crouched even lower over Glory's neck. "He's talking to him!" Cindy cried. "He's asking him for more speed!"

"Look at Glory go!" Samantha threw her hands in the air.

Cindy hadn't thought it possible for a horse to go faster than Glory already was, but the gray colt found another gear. Changing leads, he opened up a twenty-five-length lead, then a thirty-length one, over Flightful.

"Cindy, the crowd is giving Glory a standing ovation!" Beth said happily.

Glory flashed under the wire, all beauty and unstoppable power in motion to Cindy—and kept going.

"We have a world record for the mile and a quarter—and a glorious winner!" the announcer exclaimed.

Felipe was trying to ease Glory, but the colt barely slowed. *He seems to want to run forever,* Cindy thought in wonder as the cheers of the crowd pounded in her ears. *I can hardly believe this is real—it's my every dream come true.*

"Oh, Cindy, what a race!" Samantha's eyes were brimming with tears of pride. "Two Breeders' Cup winners for Whitebrook!"

"I know, it's just too incredible!" Cindy hugged her older sister tightly.

"Let's go get our champ!" Ian yelled over the deafening noise.

Felipe rode Glory through the gap, waving his crop in triumph.

"Glory, oh, Glory!" Cindy cried. The colt's neck was dark with sweat, but his eyes were bright and he was tossing his head. At her words Glory's ears pricked and his dark eyes searched for her.

Laughing, Cindy pushed through the crowded winner's circle to her horse. "Boy, you did it!" she cried. "You've won the Classic, and you did it so fast! No one is ever going to forget you!"

The gray colt dropped his head to nuzzle her hair, blowing hot breaths. Then he rubbed his nose against her shoulder, seeming to eat up the praise. Felipe quickly dismounted.

"I really didn't know how fast he was going or I might have tried harder to rate him." Felipe shook his head. "I only saw the numbers on the board as we were coming down the stretch. He was going so easily, I just let him keep it up."

"Glory set a track record for that eighth of a mile after the race, too, when you were trying to pull him up." Mike shook his head. "Absolutely amazing."

"Glory ran as fast as in my dream," Cindy said happily. "Like he had wings."

Ashleigh, Mike, and Ian turned to respond to the reporters' shouted questions. Cindy tried to position Glory straight for the winner's photo, but as with Shining, it wasn't easy. The colt was dancing around in a circle and shaking his head. "You're as pleased with yourself as everyone else is," Cindy said. "But stand still, Glory! This picture is important."

At last Glory stood dead still, ears pricked. Cindy relaxed, smiling for the cameras. Mike and Ashleigh stood beside her, as did Ian and Beth. Glory wouldn't be there without the teamwork of every one of them, Cindy realized—and that of Samantha as well.

"Where's Sammy?" Cindy whispered to Ashleigh. Cindy felt some of her joy fade. *Sammy's so important to me*, Cindy thought. *I can't feel good about Glory's win unless Sammy's here to share it*. Cindy wondered if Samantha had second thoughts about celebrating Glory's victory.

Ashleigh grinned. "Just wait and see where Sammy is," she said. "I think you'll like this, Cindy."

"Here she comes!" a photographer called, and the cameras started clicking like mad.

Cindy looked around in the mob to see who they could possibly be talking about and saw—Shining! Samantha was leading the roan filly back to the winner's circle. Shining had been sponged and cooled out, and she wore a clean saddle cloth and racing saddle over her sleek roan coat.

"The track officials thought it would make a good shot to have our two horses together," Samantha said, beaming with pride. "It's not every day that a stable has two Breeders' Cup winners!"

"How did you get Shining up here so fast?" Cindy asked happily.

Samantha winked. "Len had her all saddled and ready. We had a feeling she'd be coming back to the winner's circle."

Shining couldn't look more gorgeous, Cindy thought as she moved Glory next to Shining for the photo. And sharing this triumph with Samantha was all Cindy could ever have wished for. "Thanks, Sammy," Cindy whispered. "You know—for everything."

"What are sisters for?" Samantha said softly.

"Hold it!" called a photographer.

I just couldn't be happier, Cindy thought, smiling broadly into the cameras.

Heather ran up to the winner's circle. "I've got it—

my sketch of Glory winning the Breeders' Cup," she said breathlessly.

"I wondered where you were!" Cindy took the sketch from Heather and looked it over. "Heather, I can't believe how good this is!" In the pencil sketch, Glory was flying across the finish line, his mane and tail flowing in line with his strides. The drawing captured perfectly Glory's grace, majesty, and beauty as he won the greatest race of his life.

Cindy looked at her friend admiringly. "You're so talented, Heather!" she said.

Heather blushed. "Thanks," she said. "I think I had a pretty good subject to draw, though."

Heather can't jump horses as well as Mandy or train them like me, but she knows how to do something with horses that neither of us can, Cindy thought. Smiling so hard her face hurt, she turned in the hubbub to see how Glory was doing—and found herself face-to-face with Joe Gallagher.

Cindy's first thought was to avoid him. But there was nowhere to go quickly, certainly not while she was holding Glory.

Joe hesitated. "Your colt had a nice run," he said abruptly to Mike and Len. "Couldn't have been better. It was nice for this old man to see." Then he disappeared into the crowd.

"Can you believe it?" Samantha asked in astonishment.

"I'm glad to have that old grudge put aside," Len said. He didn't sound surprised.

"A lot of old grudges have been put aside today." Ashleigh smiled. "It feels good."

"Yeah, it does," Mike agreed.

Lavinia Townsend pushed through the crowd toward the thickest gathering of reporters.

"Oh, no—look who's here," Heather whispered to Cindy.

Cindy laughed. "I don't think we have to worry about her too much anymore," she whispered back.

"What's next for Glory after today's world record?" called a reporter.

"We'll consider a winter campaign in Florida for him," Lavinia said.

Cindy opened her mouth to object. What was Lavinia talking about? Glory was coming back to Whitebrook for the winter! Then Cindy saw Ashleigh shaking her head.

I know what that means—let Lavinia say whatever she wants, and don't argue with her. We'll do it our way later. Watching Lavinia try to answer the reporters' questions to keep the attention on herself, Cindy thought she understood Lavinia now. They might never be friends, but Cindy didn't think what Lavinia did would bother her anymore.

"If a Florida campaign isn't feasible, we'll consider retiring the colt to stud," Brad announced.

What? Cindy stared at him incredulously. *That's the first any of us have heard about that!*

"Brad—" Ashleigh drew an impatient breath.

Cindy winced, expecting the sharp words to fly. She didn't like Brad or agree with him that Glory should race again so soon or retire. But she wished Brad and Ashleigh didn't have to fight, not now, when it was such a happy day.

Ashleigh let out her breath slowly. "Glory will race a four-year-old season, probably starting with the Donn Handicap in February, but first he'll have a good rest," she said firmly, turning to the reporters. "All Glory's co-owners have already agreed to that. Remember, Brad?"

Brad seemed about to protest, but at that moment Glory whinnied long and shrilly, as if to say, *You'd better believe I'll be back next year!*

Brad frowned. Then he shrugged and turned again to the group of reporters.

"Let's get another photo with our Horse of the Year before we cool him out," Ashleigh said. Samantha moved Shining in closer to Glory and put her arm around Cindy.

The gray colt whinnied again and nudged Cindy hard with his nose, asking for the attention he deserved so much. Cindy laughed from sheer joy. "I know you'll be back next year," she said. "And nobody could have said it better."

Joanna Campbell was born and raised in Norwalk, Connecticut and grew up loving horses. She eventually owned a horse of her own and took riding lessons for a number of years, specializing in jumping. She still rides when possible and has started her three-year-old granddaughter on lessons. In addition to publishing over twenty-five novels for young adults, she is the author of four adult novels. She has also sung and played piano professionally and owned an antique business. She now lives on the coast of Maine in Camden with her husband, Ian Bruce. She has two children, Kimberly and Kenneth, and three grand-children.

Karen Bentley rode in English equitation and jumping classes as a child and in Western equitation and barrel racing classes as a teenager. She has bred and raised Quarter Horses and, during a sojourn on the East Coast, owned a half-Thoroughbred jumper. She now owns a red roan registered Quarter Horse with some reining moves and lives in New Mexico. She has published nine novels for young adults.